MW00918151

FOREST GUARD

DARK CORPS
-SPECIAL MISSIONS-

WOLF SQUAD: BLACKOUT

DARK CORPS
- BOOK 4 -

FOREST GUARD

CAMERON ALEXANDER

BICKERING
OWLS
PUBLISHING

To an amazing artist and
guiding light for Dark Corps,
thanks Rhett!
--Cameron

Right back to you, Cameron!
Both you and your saga are EPIC!
Thanks for keeping me around.
--Rhett

Dark Corps series. Forest Guard
by Cameron Alexander
Published by Bickering Owls Publishing

Copyright: Cameron Alexander
Illustrations: ©Bickering Owls Publishing

All rights reserved.
No portion of this book may be reproduced
in any form without permission from the publisher,
except as permitted by U.S. copyright law.
For permission contact:
dmaracle@bickeringowls.com

Art and Book Design by Rhett Pennell

ISBN: 978-1-7321056-0-7
First Printing   March 2018

CONTENTS

PROLOGUE

This is a story about a boy named Timmy Barnes and his five stuffed bears that wear armor and use weapons that shoot pure light to fight off an army of shadowy creatures called the Dark. Bear Company's mission is to return Timmy to his father, a world-famous scientist named Dr. Barnes, in order to ultimately save the world from Total Dark.

If that paragraph was at all confusing to you, it means either you haven't read the first three books in this series, or you have a very poor memory. If it's the first part—that you haven't read the first three Dark Corps books—then I strongly suggest that you go back and do that, and I also suggest you be quick about it, because I'm going to continue telling this story whether you're here or not. If it's the second part and you simply have a very poor memory, I'm afraid I can't really help you with that, other than to suggest that you eat lots of vegetables and get a full eight hours of sleep at night (which is actually good advice for anyone, whether you have a poor memory or not).

Where was I? Oh, that's right. Normally this is the part of the book where I would give you a recap, which is short for "recapitulation," which is just a fancy way of saying "a reminder of everything that has happened so far." However, so many fantastical things have happened to Timmy and Bear Company on their incredible journey so far that it would likely take me this entire book just to tell you about everything, and that would be no good at all because we wouldn't get anywhere with *this* story. So instead, I'll simply remind you where we last saw Timmy, Anna, Glen, and the five bears, and then we'll continue right along.

After they escaped from the city with the help of Wolf Squad, Bear Company brought Timmy and Anna to an old farm, where they spent a truly frightening night fighting off the Dark while trapped in a barn. Lucky for them, they had the assistance of the Homestead Defense Force and they were able to escape. Bear Company thought they were out of the woods (which is just a saying that means "out of harm's way," since they had not yet actually gone into the woods, though they would soon) but they were attacked by the biggest, meanest Dark they had ever seen, a terrible shadow named Dark Cloud.

The bears managed to defeat Dark Cloud, and as morning came they headed into the woods (see? I told you) towards the next stage of their remarkable voyage.

Except there was just one teeny, tiny problem: Dark Cloud was defeated, but he was not gone. You see, Bear Company thought that they had destroyed the shadow with their flashers, the weapons on their wrists that fired pure light. But instead, Dark Cloud had spread his shadow out as wide as he could, blending in with the darkness of the night so that the bears only *thought* that he was gone.

The Dark were creatures made of the darkest, blackest shadows, and they could bond with everyday objects and make it a part of them. For example, a Dark could bond with a tennis racket, and then they might have a tennis racket for an arm—which wouldn't actually be all that useful, unless they were practicing their backswing, but I'm sure you get the idea.

Dark Cloud was the best of all the Dark at bonding with things, perhaps even better than Total Dark, the leader of the shadowy creatures from another world. And in that very early morning air, after the bears had blasted Dark Cloud to pieces, he was desperate to bond with anything to keep him from evaporating forever. There was only one thing around—a fine, misty fog hanging over the field where the battle had taken place.

In case you didn't know, fog is made up of very tiny droplets of water, so small you can't even see them, so tiny that they actually hang in the air very close together. And as I mentioned, Dark Cloud was excellent at bonding with things. Even though he was grievously injured ("grievously" being a fancy way of saying "very, very seriously") he stuck what was left of his shadow to these millions and millions of teeny-tiny-itsy-bitsy water droplets and bonded with the early morning fog.

Over the course of several minutes, Dark Cloud became very much a literal dark cloud, his shadow hanging in the air and made mostly of water vapor. Now this was both good and bad for him—it was good, because it meant that he could survive for at least a little while longer and maybe even gain back some of his strength if he was given enough time. However, it was also bad, because water vapor is little more than a gas, which meant that he couldn't really hurt anyone or anything with his dark cloud body.

(And I'm sure you can see how what is good and bad for Dark Cloud is also bad and good for Bear Company.)

Dark Cloud needed time to heal, and morning was coming fast. By the time he was done bonding with the fog around him, the sky was turning from purple to blue, and soon the sun would be up. The Dark could not survive in direct sunlight; during the day they had to stick to shadowy nooks and dark crannies. He needed somewhere to hide, and the forest seemed as good a place as any. Maybe the large, thick trees would provide him some shade and safety from the sun.

His vast, shapeless black-fog body drifted towards the woods, gathering even more fog as he traveled and becoming very massive. "*I'll get you yet, boy*," he hissed to himself. "*I will bond with your bears and become the most powerful*

Dark of all!"

Dark Cloud's foggy body drifted over something—an object lying in the grass. It was a canister of chemicals, and on one side of the can was a white painted skull. Dark Cloud had bonded with it during the battle at the barn, but it had fallen when the bears blasted him with their flashers. He tested his strength, trying to bond with the can. It was hard work, since he was so weak, but eventually the canister floated up into his shadowy fog. The painted skull on the outside of the can looked as if it was his face, and he hissed a small greenish cloud with each breath.

Then he headed straight for the forest.

CHAPTER 1:

INTO THE WOODS

"**I** really don't see what all the fuss is about," Bruiser grumbled as he sat on the mossy floor of the forest with his back to a large spruce tree. Bruiser was the green bear of Bear Company. He was very good at fighting; in fact, it was his favorite thing to do. His second-favorite thing to do, as you can guess, was to grumble, grouse, groan, or otherwise complain about everything.

"Just sit still and let Patch take a look at you," Mother told him gently. She was the leader of Bear Company, and her armor was a shiny red that was quite bright in the sunlight. It was her job to keep the bears moving towards their goal of returning Timmy to his father. She knew how to deal with each bear, and the best way to deal with Bruiser's complaining was usually with sharp scolding—but in this case, she chose to be more gentle, because the green bear was injured.

"Hmm," said Patch thoughtfully. She stood on her knees and leaned over, inspecting Bruiser's belly. "Sorry, Bruiser, but I'm not sure I can fix this. I have the tools, but we don't have the spare parts." Patch was the yellow bear, and the medic of Bear Company. She could fix up anyone, from robotic toy bears to humans and even real live animals—as long as she had the parts.

During the fight in the field against Dark

Cloud, as morning was coming, Bruiser had taken a direct hit to his armored belly. Dark Cloud had bonded with a scythe, which is a long, curved blade that is usually used for cutting down stalks of grain—but the Dark used it as a weapon against Bear Company. Bruiser was okay, but there was a long gash in the front of his armor, exposing his plushy green belly underneath it.

You see, each of the bears was once an ordinary stuffed toy—at least, they *looked* like an ordinary stuffed toy. Each time Timmy and his father moved to a new place (which was a lot) Dr. Barnes would give his son a new set of stuffed animals. Sometimes they were farm animals; other times they were jungle beasts or a pack of wolves or large birds of prey. Each time they moved, Timmy would somehow lose the last set of stuffed animals. His father would say things like, "Oh, the movers must have misplaced that box," or "I'm sorry, Timmy, I could have sworn I packed them with the rest of your toys." And each time they arrived somewhere new, there would be a new set of stuffed animals. The last time they moved, when they came to the city, Dr. Barnes had given Timmy the five stuffed bears, each one a different color.

And that was the last time Timmy had seen his dad.

Now Timmy understood why he had "lost" his stuffed toys with each new move. Each set of animals was a unit of the Dark Corps, and each set was built by Dr. Barnes to protect Timmy in case something terrible happened. Normally they looked very much like regular old stuffed animals, except that each one of them had a hard metal case on its back. And when they were activated by Dr. Barnes, only a few days ago, the metal cases sprang open to reveal the shining armor that covered their soft bodies, and they began to walk and talk and fight off the Dark and sometimes even make jokes.

"Timmy," Mother called out. "Don't wander too far. These woods are deep. It would be easy to get lost."

"I won't get lost," Timmy promised.

As morning came, the eight of them—the five bears and three children—had entered the forest and began making their way through. Mother said that there was a river on the other side, and that was their next rendezvous point. Timmy had heard that word several times on their journey so far, so he knew that "rendezvous point" was a phrase that meant "a place where you meet up with others," but he couldn't help wonder how many rendezvous points they would have to travel to before he saw his dad again. It already felt like they had gone very far, but he didn't feel any closer to the end.

At least they were out of the city and away from the farm, Timmy thought. In the daytime, the woods seemed pleasant and welcoming. There was a nice smell to the trees that reminded Timmy of when he was younger and he and his dad lived on the edge of a forest. They would take long walks together and talk about all sorts of things, like the patterns of stars and combustion engines and how Styrofoam is made and what's really in hot dogs. Timmy wondered if this might even be the same forest.

"That's strange," said Blue quietly. He was standing near Timmy, looking up towards the canopy (which is a fancy term for the ceiling of leaves that the trees formed over their heads) and his shiny blue ears were twitching left and right. He was the computer expert of Bear Company, and also the one that held their map and the radio.

His real name was Keylogger, but Timmy (and the other bears) just called him Blue.

"What's strange?" Timmy asked.

"My map is all fuzzy," Blue replied. His eyes shined a little brighter as he tried to look at the GPS map in his helmet. "I think it's this thick canopy of leaves… it must be blocking our signal."

"We don't need a map," Sneak insisted. "I have a great sense of direction." Sneak was the orange bear, and the scout of Bear Company. He was very, very sneaky and could move without making a sound—except that there was a problem with his hardware and he sometimes let out a random, high-pitched noise that sounded like part hiccup and part sneeze.

"I'm sure you have an excellent sense of direction," said Blue, "but that doesn't help us if we don't know which direction we need to go."

"Hmm," said Sneak. "That is a problem."

"Blue, try the radio," Mother told him. "See if we can get Corps Command to help us find our way."

While Blue tried to call the General on the radio, Timmy wandered over to his new friends, Anna and Glen. Anna was an orphan girl that Bear Company had rescued from the Dark while they were still in the city. She didn't have anywhere else to go, so she decided to tag along with Timmy and the bears. She was brave and liked to laugh a lot. Having Anna around usually made Timmy feel braver too.

"I'm getting hungry," Anna said, rubbing her empty stomach. "I hope we can find something to eat soon."

"I'll bet I can catch us a rabbit!" Glen offered.

Glen was a boy who lived on the farm where Dark Cloud and his minions had attacked.

He was trying to find his family, who he had lost when the power went out. Glen was very resourceful, which is a fancy way of saying that he was clever and creative. "All I need is a box, and some twine, and a carrot."

"We don't have a box," Anna said. "Or any twine."

"And if we had a carrot," Timmy added, "We would probably just eat it."

"Besides, there's no way I would eat a poor little bunny rabbit!" said Anna.

"Are you sure?" Glen teased. "They're very tasty."

Anna stuck out her tongue and made a face.

"We're not catching any rabbits," Mother said as she came over. "And we're certainly not eating them. Don't worry, kids. We'll find some food soon, I promise." Even though she sounded like she was certain, inside she wasn't so sure. It would be very hard to find the river without the map, and it would be very hard for the children to keep moving if they didn't find food soon. But everyone looked to Mother to lead them, so she had to do her best to keep everyone as calm and happy as she could. "Blue?" she asked. "How's it going with the radio?"

"Not good." He shook his head. "We have no signal."

"That's okay," said Mother, even though it wasn't the truth. "We'll find our way. I'm certain it's this direction. Come on, Bear Company— let's move!"

CHAPTER 2:

THE SILVER SQUIRREL

Dark Cloud felt very strange. He felt as if he was detached from his body, like his mind was somehow separate from the foggy shadow that he now was. He could not even see how large he had become. But at the same time, if he concentrated very hard, he could still feel distant parts of him—he somehow knew that there was a massive oak tree about two hundred feet from his chemical-canister head, even though he could not see it. He somehow knew that this tree had been split by lightning and was now mostly dead and hollow in the center. He knew it by feeling it, because he was so large at this point that the edges of his dark cloud were two hundred feet away.

Dark Cloud had never taken a science class before, or else he might have understood what he had become. You probably know this already, but all matter in the whole world is made up of tiny, tiny little particles called molecules, and the way these molecules move around each other tells us the state of matter—that is, if something is a solid, a liquid, or a gas.

When something is solid, like a tea kettle or a cardboard box, the molecules are very close together, packed in there tightly like a crowded elevator. The molecules have nowhere to go, so they vibrate against each other very quickly. When something is a liquid, the molecules have a little bit more space, and they can slip and slide past each other, which is why water flows or spills out into a puddle. Lastly, when something is a gas, it's like the molecules are in a wide open field—they have plenty of room to move about, and they zip around at high speeds without worrying much about bumping into each other. That's why smoke from a fire just drifts away into the air without taking on any shape; because the molecules have all the space in the world to float away.

Of course, Dark Cloud didn't know anything about states of matter or molecules or even crowded elevators, but if he did, he might understand that the reason he felt so detached was because his body was little more than a gas right now. He had stretched himself to the very limits of what a Dark could do. Only a small part of his now-very-large shadow was anything close to solid, and that was the part that bonded with his chemical-canister head and its painted white skull, puffing small gusts of green poison like cold breaths.

What he *did* know, however, was that this newfound skill of being able to "feel" parts of him from far away could be very useful in finding the bears. But now it was light out, and he needed shelter from the sun. Even though the leaves above him were thick, the sunlight could still hurt him. He slithered very low to the ground, as close to the dirt and moss as he could, and quickly made his way towards the hollowed-out tree. He squeezed as much of his shadow into it as he could, and the rest floated around it, safe for now from the sunlight.

There were no people around to see it, but if

there were, they probably would have been very frightened to see an old, dead tree with black fog slowly drifting all around it. They would have thought that it looked like something right out a scary movie. They probably would have called the police, or maybe they would have contacted their nearest dendrologist (which is a *very* fancy term for a person who studies trees), or at the very least, they would have run screaming for their life.

But there were no people around to see it. And though there may not have been any people, there was something—a squirrel, several trees away, sitting in a high branch of a tall tree. The squirrel clung to the very thin branch with her tiny hands, using her wide tail to balance herself, as squirrels do. But this was no ordinary squirrel.

She stared at the strange, dead tree and noticed the dark fog rolling slowly from inside

it and all around it. Her bright, lavender-colored eyes made a whirring sound as she focused on the oak tree and magnified it. From here, she could not see exactly what it was, but she knew that something was not right about it. She had to tell the others.

She turned and scurried quickly down the branch. When she reached the end of it, the squirrel jumped right off, soaring through the air and flattening her great silver tail, which slowed her down enough to grab onto the branch of another tree. She leapt from branch to branch this way, moving as quickly and easily as her name suggested—which was Nimble.

If Dark Cloud had not been hiding from the sun in the dead tree, he might have noticed a flash of her silver tail or a blur of glowing lavender eyes as the armored squirrel darted through the forest, but he was too busy trying to keep his shadow away from the light. He would wait there until it was dark, he decided.

And then he would find the bears.

CHAPTER 3:

A 100% CHANCE WE'RE LOST

Timmy's legs felt heavy. He kept telling himself that it would not be much further, that soon they would find the river and be on the next part of their journey. Two times already they had heard the sound of rushing water and excitedly ran towards it, only to find a small stream or tiny waterfall instead. His stomach gurgled; he was very hungry now, and he had not slept in the last two nights.

He could tell that the other two children, Anna and Glen, felt the same way that he did. They trudged along, dragging their feet across the dirt and moss as they continued through the never-ending forest.

Mother tried her best to be cheerful. "I'm sure it's not much further now!" she said loudly. "I bet there's lots of fish in the river, too. Do you like fish, Anna?"

Anna wrinkled her nose. "Not unless you're hiding some tartar sauce or ketchup in that metal case on your back."

Blue kept trying the radio, but all it did was make a hissing noise that sounded like *tsssshhhhht*. Even Bruiser couldn't keep up his grumbling; he was too sour to complain about being sour.

"Hey Timmy," said Patch. "Did you hear the

joke about the German sausage?" Patch had a habit of telling bad jokes when she was nervous, and right now she was very nervous that they were terribly lost in the woods. "It was the wurst!"

Even though that is a very funny joke, likely one of the best you'll ever hear, no one laughed on account of being so tired, hungry, sour, or some combination of those things.

Mother knew that she couldn't expect the children to keep going like this. They needed a plan. She paused and glanced upward, towards the tops of the trees. In case you didn't know, bears are excellent tree-climbers. (They're also very good swimmers and they can run quite fast, all of which is good to know if you ever find yourself being chased by a bear. In fact, the best thing to do in that situation would be to stop and tell the bear the joke about the German sausage, because the bear will be too busy laughing to chase you any farther.)

"Sneak, do you think you could get up to the top of this tree and see if you can peek over the canopy?" Mother asked. "Maybe you'll be able to see the river from up there."

"Sure thing..." Sneak started to say, but Bruiser shoved him aside.

"I'll do it!" the green bear shouted. "I'm bored out of my mind with all this walking. Let me climb it!"

"No way!" Sneak shouted. "Mother asked *me* to do it. Besides, you're hurt."

Bruiser laughed. "Hurt? It's just a crack in my armor. Big deal. I'm still a better climber than you—"

"That's enough!" Mother said sharply. "Sneak, climb the tree. Bruiser, stand there and be quiet or I'll demote you to Bear Company's janitor!"

"Yes, ma'am," Bruiser grumbled.

"Ha, you got in trouble," Sneak teased as he started to climb the tree. He shimmied easily up the trunk until he could reach the lowest branches, and then began to climb up as easily as if he was on a ladder. He was a good climber, but the higher he got, the thinner the branches became, and the more nervous Timmy was to watch him.

"Is he going to be okay?" Anna asked. She was standing right next to Timmy and clearly she was thinking the same thing.

"Probably not," said a quiet voice between them. "There's an 84.6 percent chance that he'll fall."

Anna gasped, but Timmy was not surprised at all to see that a small yellow rabbit had joined them. Even with its long ears, it stood only two feet tall, and its yellow armor was darker in some places with a swirling camouflage pattern. To any normal person, seeing an armored rabbit with glowing yellow eyes suddenly appear right beside you would seem very strange, but after meeting Bear Company, Air Strike, Wolf Squad, and the Homestead Defense Force, Timmy was getting used to these sorts of things.

So instead of saying "what are you?" or "how are you able to speak?" or screaming, "aaaaaaaaaaaaaaaahhhhhhh!!" Timmy just said, "Hello."

"Hello," said the rabbit. "Sorry to sneak up on you. I figured there was a 74.2 percent chance that you wouldn't hear me, on account of being distracted."

"Lucky!" Mother said, only just now noticing the rabbit. "Thank goodness you found us. I was beginning to think we were lost… um, I mean, of course we weren't lost. But still. It's good to see you."

"Good to see you too, Mother," said the rabbit, apparently named Lucky. "Do you remember me, Timmy? I figure there's about a 64.7 percent chance that you do."

Timmy thought for a long moment. "Yes... I do remember you. My dad gave me a stuffed rabbit when we lived at the edge of the woods. It was you and... some other woodland creatures, right?"

"We prefer to be called the Forest Guard, but yes. That's right."

Timmy tried hard to remember what other animals had been a part of the set. There was a rabbit (clearly), and a fox, and a squirrel, and... he couldn't remember who else.

"Wait a second," said Anna. "Did you say something about a chance that Sneak would fall?"

"I did," said Lucky. "An 84.6 percent chance, to be precise."

Suddenly there was a loud *crack* from above them as a tree branch broke. Then there was a shout of surprise, and a moment later Sneak landed on the soft moss at the base of the tree with a stupendous *thud!*

"Are you okay?!" Anna asked, helping the bear up.

"Ooh… yeah, I think so," said Sneak, rubbing his orange head.

"How did you know that?" Glen asked the rabbit.

"Dr. Barnes built me with a probability calculator," Lucky answered.

"I don't know what that means," Timmy admitted.

"It means that he's really lucky," Bruiser

grumbled.

"No, it means that I can calculate the chances that something is going to happen before it happens," Lucky explained. "So it only *looks* like I'm very lucky. But really I'm just Lucky."

Timmy was fairly confused, but he nodded anyway. He looked the rabbit over and couldn't help but notice that his flasher was different from Bear Company's flashers. Lucky's flasher had a slightly different shape and a longer barrel. But he decided not to say anything about it, because he was sure that Bruiser would be jealous of it.

Lucky turned to Mother. "You should come with me to our safe house. It's not far. We can wait for the others there."

"What's a safe house?" Glen asked.

"It's a secret place where we can hide out," Blue explained.

"But why would we need to hide out?" asked

Timmy. "Are there any Dark here in the woods?"

"I figure there's a very small chance that any Dark followed you," said Lucky. "Somewhere around 8.3 percent. But even so, we're not doing ourselves any favors sitting out in the open like this. We can talk more when we reach the safe house. Follow me… It's this way!" The small yellow rabbit bounded forward, hopping on his large feet and using his hands for balance. Anna followed, and then Glen, Timmy, and Bear Company.

CHAPTER 4:

THE SAFE HOUISE

"This is your secret place?" Glen asked. "Your safe house?"

"It looks… cozy," said Anna slowly.

"It looks like a dump," Bruiser groaned.

The safe house, as Lucky called it, was a small log cabin in the woods, barely much bigger than a two-car garage. It didn't look like anyone had been there for a long time. The logs were gray and rotting away in some places. The black shingles on the roof had turned green from moss and mildew and were curling upward, peeling away from the wood. There were only two windows, and they were so grimy that it was impossible to see inside.

"Hey, don't worry," Patch said quietly to Timmy. "Things aren't always how they seem at first. Remember that storage unit in the city?"

"Yes, I do." Timmy remembered it well. From the outside it had looked like just a regular old storage unit filled with old junk, but inside was the secret weapons cache where Bear Company got their flashers. Patch was right; Timmy was certain the inside of the ramshackle cabin would probably be full of wondrous gadgets and high-tech gizmos.

He was wrong.

Lucky yanked open the door with a grunt

and the hinges creaked loudly. "Sorry," the rabbit said, "but the door sticks sometimes… about 59.6 percent of the time, to be exact." The inside of the cabin smelled musty and felt damp. The walls were the same gray color as the logs outside—there had been wallpaper on them at some point, but now it was peeling and impossible to tell what color it might have been. There were only three rooms; one was a large common room with a fireplace, and another was a small bedroom in the back. The third room was a tiny bathroom.

"Whose cabin is this?" Anna asked.

"We're not sure," said Lucky. "We don't think it belongs to anyone anymore. If it does, they haven't been here in a long time."

Glen shivered a little. "This looks like a cabin from a movie I saw once."

"I hope it was a nice movie," Timmy said,

even though he was sure it was not.

"It was about these five kids that went into the woods to stay at a cabin just like this one, and then this crazy guy with an axe came and—"

"Okay!" said Mother loudly. "I think that's about enough of that. Lucky, is there any electricity here?"

"Sorry, no," said the rabbit. "But there is a small generator in the back, in case you need to charge your flashers."

"How about running water?" Anna asked. "I could really use a shower."

"No such luck," said Lucky. "But we should have some bottles around somewhere—"

Suddenly the door to the small bedroom creaked open. Timmy jumped a little.

"Ah, you're here!" An orange raccoon, about the same height as the bears and with ornage-colored eyes, greeted them. "I'm glad to see you all! Lucky said there was a high probability you'd get lost."

"We did get lost," Sneak admitted. "Sort of."

"Well, I can't imagine what you've been through so far," said the raccoon. "Fighting off a whole army of Dark to get to us! It's truly amazing."

"How do you know about that, Pilfer?" Blue asked. "Our radios don't work in the forest."

"That's true," said the raccoon. "Sly leaves the forest once each day to call Corps Command and get updates. They told us you were on your way, so we had Lucky and Nimble keeping an eye out for you. Hang on a second—I have something for you kids."

The raccoon, called Pilfer, disappeared back into the small bedroom and came back with a black nylon satchel over one of his shoulders. ("Satchel," by the way, is just a fancy word for "sack," but since "satchel" sounds much more official and proper, we'll use that instead of boring old "sack.") He dropped the satchel in the center of the room, loosened the drawstring, and started pulling out items and setting them on the wooden floor.

"Let's see," he said. "We've got baked beans, canned ravioli, fruit cups, instant noodles, bottled water..." Pilfer pulled out a can opener, a small camp stove, a canister of propane, some candles, a book of matches, and a flashlight. "I think this should get us through the night, don't you?"

"Wow," said Anna quietly. Her stomach rumbled loudly. Timmy was thinking the same thing—normally it wouldn't seem like much, but they were so hungry that it looked like Thanksgiving dinner.

"Wait a second," said Mother. "What do you

mean, 'get us through the night'? What about the river?"

"Oh," said Lucky, "the river's too far away to get to before sundown. And even though there's only an 8.3 percent chance that there's any Dark out there, Stag still thought it would be best for the children to eat and get some rest before we continue on."

"Besides," Pilfer added, "if we wait for the others, then we can all go together. There's strength in numbers, right?"

"Right," Mother agreed, but she said it quietly, which made Timmy think that she didn't really agree at all. He understood why. After everything they had been through so far, he would have preferred to get to the river as quickly as possible too. And he *really* didn't want to spend the night in this tumbledown cabin.

Anna and Pilfer were already setting up

the camp stove. "Excuse me," she said to the raccoon. "I don't mean to be rude, but... how did you get all this stuff?"

"Oh," said Pilfer, "I borrowed it."

"You *borrowed* it?" said Anna with a small laugh. "You can't borrow food!"

"Sure you can," Pilfer insisted. "There are some homes on the other side of the woods. I snuck inside, and I left detailed drawings of everything I took, with the letters 'I.O.U.' on them."

"Wait a second," said Glen, "doesn't pilfer mean 'to steal'?"

"What?" The small orange raccoon looked very confused. "That's preposterous! Pilfer is my name. It doesn't mean anything other than that."

"Pilfer is the Forest Guard's expert thief," Lucky said quietly to Timmy. "See, your dad knew that Corps Command might need an expert thief, to pick locks and occasionally take things. But he also knew that stealing is dishonest, and that the Dark Corps always does the right thing. That's why Pilfer doesn't think of himself as a thief."

"So… will he really return all those things he took?" Timmy asked.

"Yup," said Lucky.

"And where will he get it from?"

"Well," said Lucky with a laugh, "he'll probably steal it from someone else."

What a strange bunch, Timmy thought, but he didn't say it out loud. Come to think of it, each unit of the Dark Corps had been slightly stranger than the last. He couldn't imagine who they might meet next—though all he really wanted was to see his dad again, and go home, and have this whole thing be over.

As the kids gathered around the camp stove to eat, Mother and Blue approached Lucky. "We'll stay the night here," Mother agreed, "but we must go as soon as it's light out."

"Definitely," said Lucky. "There's only a 17.2 percent chance of rain tomorrow, so we should have an easy journey to the river."

"And you haven't seen any Dark in the forest yet?" Blue asked.

"Not a single one," said Lucky. "We've been… well, we've been lucky, I suppose."

"That's a relief," said Mother. Even though she didn't like the idea of spending the night in the cabin, she *did* like the idea of having at least one night when they weren't being attacked by the Dark. It would be good for the children to eat and get some sleep and start again fresh in the morning.

"Hey!" Bruiser shouted suddenly. He

marched over to Pilfer, grabbed the raccoon's small arm, and pulled it up into the air so that everyone could see. "What is *this*?"

"Oh, my flasher?" said Pilfer. "What's wrong with it?"

"It's… it's…" Bruiser couldn't seem to form the right words. "Well… it's better than mine!" Pilfer's flasher, much like Lucky's, had a slightly longer barrel and looked a little more advanced than the ones that Bear Company had.

"Oh, I see," said Pilfer. "You've still got the *old* flashers. These are the model-two flashers. They have a longer range, and they fire three times faster! Best of all, they're solar-powered. That's why we've been calling them solar flares. They're nice, right?"

"Well… yes!" Bruiser grumbled. "Of course they're nice! And now I want one too!"

CHAPTER 5:

NOT VERY HAPPY

Ms. Gertrude was not very happy. Not even a little bit. If you remember Ms. Gertrude, then that won't be at all surprising, because Ms. Gertrude was never really happy—but today, she was even more unhappy than usual.

For the last month or so, Ms. Gertrude had been the nanny for the Barnes family, a famous scientist named Peter and his young son Timothy.

While Dr. Barnes was away working on some top-secret project, it was Ms. Gertrude's job to cook Timothy's meals and do the laundry, to keep the house clean and make sure he brushed his teeth. She did all of those things, though she never smiled and she never whistled while she worked and she never once ever said, "Good night, sleep tight, don't let the bedbugs bite." In fact, most nights, she simply said "lights out!" and closed Timmy's bedroom door.

Timmy had always thought it was kind of strange that Ms. Gertrude didn't look anything at all like a nanny. She always wore black slacks and a black blazer and a crisp white shirt. Her nose was sharp and a little crooked, because it had been broken before and didn't quite heal right, and her hair was always in a very tight bun on the top of her head.

The reason that Ms. Gertrude didn't look

anything like a nanny at all was because she *wasn't* actually a nanny at all. Sure, she did the jobs that a nanny would do, like cooking and cleaning and laundry, but that was just her cover (which is a fancy term for disguise). Ms. Gertrude had only pretended to be Timmy Barnes's nanny, because she was actually an agent with a very top-secret organization, and her organization was keeping Dr. Barnes in an underground base while he worked on their very top-secret project of building a portal to another world. The agency knew that someone needed to watch over Timmy, just in case the doctor refused to build the portal, so they chose Ms. Gertrude.

And if you knew anything about Ms. Gertrude, you would probably find that somewhat funny, because Ms. Gertrude didn't even like children very much.

But none of that was the reason that Ms.

Gertrude wasn't very happy today. The real reason that Ms. Gertrude was so unhappy was because Timothy Barnes had vanished from his bed three nights ago. He ran away from home and left her a note that said he was going to find his father. The strangest part, though, was that he took his five stuffed bears with him.

And now, Ms. Gertrude's new job was to find Timmy.

So far she had tracked him all over the city and found nothing except strange stories about talking bears and shadows that moved all on their own. Next she followed the trail out to the countryside. She was driving by a cornfield when she noticed that a bunch of the tall stalks had been trampled flat. She followed the new path of crumpled corn to an old farmhouse, but there was no one home. There was, however, a tractor sitting near the house and, curiously, the engine was slightly smoking—which meant that someone had been there recently.

Past the tractor was a barn. Ms. Gertrude went inside and saw that the doors were broken and there was a gaping hole in the roof. The rear wall of the barn had been broken through by… something. It looked like some sort of battle had taken place there.

"Strange," Ms. Gertrude muttered to herself. "What on earth could have happened here?" She had no idea—but she was certain it had something to do with Timothy Barnes, and she was equally certain that he was not here anymore. There were only two ways he could have gone from the old farmhouse: down the single road that led to the suburbs, or through the wide field behind the barn. It was unlikely that he would be on the road, because it would be too easy for someone to spot him, and a ten-year-old boy walking on a road alone might look strange to most adults.

Ms. Gertrude hiked halfway across the field before she found more strange things. There was a scythe and a sledgehammer just lying in the grass. As she kneeled over to take a closer look, another object glinted in the sunlight. She picked it up and turned it over in her hands. It was a tiny metal shard, just a sliver of bright green and slightly curved. She had no way of knowing that it was a small piece of Bruiser's broken armor, but it looked important, so she put it in her pocket.

She put one hand over her eyebrows to shield her eyes from the sun and looked left and right. *Which way would Timmy have gone?* she wondered.

Aha! She could see the edge of a forest on the far side of the field. What better place for a ten-year-old boy to hide than in the woods? She was sure that Timmy was somewhere in there, and she was very sure that she would find him.

Ms. Gertrude walked back to her car and got a flashlight out of the glove compartment. It would be dark soon, and while she was certainly not afraid of the dark, she didn't want to trip on any roots or stones and ruin her crisp white shirt.

Next, she snatched up her purse and dug around inside it until she found a small, round makeup compact, the type that flipped open and had a mirror on one side—except when she flipped it open, it wasn't a mirror at all, but a small screen. And instead of showing a reflection of her face, the small screen flickered and came to life with the image of a man in a black suit and dark sunglasses.

"This is Gertrude," she said into the small communicator.

"Report," said the man in sunglasses.

"I'm still on the trail of Timothy Barnes," she told the man. "I'm about to follow a lead. Have you been able to trace any radio signals?"

"We were locked onto a signal," said the man flatly, "but we lost it. It's as if they just vanished."

Ms. Gertrude looked up at the forest in the distance. From here, the trees looked very small, but she was sure they were actually quite large, and their thick leaves probably blocked any signal from coming through.

"Just as I suspected," she murmured.

"There's something more," said the man in the dark suit. "One of our rookie agents claims to have information on Barnes... and other things."

"What kind of other things?" Ms. Gertrude asked suspiciously.

"Something about Ice Base Delta, and these reports of shadows and talking bears," the man said. "He says that he'll only talk to the agent on the case… and that's you. So we're sending him to your location."

"What?" Ms. Gertrude did not want a partner, and she certainly didn't want some young know-it-all agent messing up her case. "Why can't he just tell me what he knows?"

"He says that he can't describe it," said the man on the small screen. "He says he has to show you. His name is Agent Reese, and he should be at your location by morning."

Ms. Gertrude groaned. "Fine. Tell him that he can show me whatever he wants… if he can find me." She snapped the small communicator shut and tossed it to the floor of her car. She took her purse and her flashlight and started towards the field. The young rookie agent would never find her in the forest, at least not before she found Timmy.

Ms. Gertrude was not very happy, and now she was even more unhappy than usual, because she was definitely not wearing the right kind of shoes for a hike through a forest.

"I'm going to find you, Timothy Barnes," she said out loud, even though there was no one else around to hear it. "And then we'll see what's really going on here."

CHAPTER 6:

THE BLACK FOG

Timmy woke with a gasp and sat up. At first he was very disoriented, which is a fancy way of saying that he wasn't sure where he was or how he had gotten there. Then he remembered: he was in the small log cabin safe house of the Forest Guard. After they had eaten, he and Anna and Glen had went to sleep in the small rear bedroom of the cabin. There was a large mattress on the floor, fitted with sheets, pillows and blankets. (Timmy really didn't want to know how Pilfer had managed to get a mattress and bed sheets and blankets, or how he planned to return them, or what those poor people that lived on the edge of the forest were sleeping on tonight.)

He was disoriented because he had been dreaming of the Dark—of inky black shadows crawling into the windows and under the doors of the cabin, seeping in like spilled oil and catching Bear Company off guard. When he woke from his dream, he still saw darkness; it was night, and without any windows in the small bedroom, it was almost pitch-black.

He reached out with his left hand and his fingers touched Glen's arm. He was still asleep, and Anna was snoring lightly on the far side of the bed. Timmy reached out with his right hand and touched something else, something plushy and warm.

"Who's there?" he whispered.

"It's me," said Mother's soft voice. "Sorry, I didn't want to startle you so I took off my armor."

"Good thinking. Thanks." Timmy would have been way more disoriented if he woke up from his nightmare and saw only a pair of red glowing eyes in the darkness.

Mother reached out and took Timmy's hand in her soft, stuffed paw. "Come with me," she whispered. He got up from the bed carefully so he didn't wake the others and followed her out of the room.

Once the door was closed behind them, Mother put her armor back on. The metal case on her back sprang open and the plates of armor slid out and over her plushy bear body with a sound like *zip-zip!*

The others—the four bears, Lucky, and

Pilfer—were all gathered around the two grimy windows at the front of the cabin, staring out into the night. Timmy knew that couldn't be a good sign. A small ball of dread formed like a heavy pit in his stomach.

"What's going on?" he asked.

"See for yourself." Patch stepped aside so Timmy could look out. At first, he saw nothing but the faint outline of trees. It was very dark out there and the moonlight was made dim by the thick canopy of leaves. But after a few seconds, his eyes adjusted, and he saw...

"What is that?" Timmy asked. "Fog?" He couldn't see the ground outside. He couldn't see the rocks or moss or the roots of the trees. The fog hung low in the air and covered everything from sight. He squinted his eyes—he was sure that the fog was moving, very slowly, drifting in low, lazy waves like the surface of the ocean.

"It's some kind of black fog," said Mother.

"I've never seen anything like this in the whole forest," said Pilfer.

"There's a zero percent chance that we know what it is," Lucky added.

"The Dark," said Timmy. "I just know it." Timmy did not have a probability calculator like Lucky did, but he was still 100 percent certain that the Dark had something to do with this black fog. The problem was that the fog didn't look like any of the Dark they had ever seen before. The Dark were creatures made of shadow, but they still had some sort of shape to them—sometimes they looked like a person, or a beast, or a bird, and one time a Dark took on the shape of a tractor it had bonded with. But this was different… there was no shape to it. There was only one way to describe it; it was like some sort of dark cloud. (Of course, at the time, Timmy had no idea how right he was about that.)

Suddenly, from between two trees came a pair of dark red glowing eyes. Timmy held his breath, his eyes wide, as a large shape slowly approached the cabin. Whatever it was, it had two tall horns on the top of its head. It looked like some sort of monster, making its way towards the cabin through the fog.

Lucky yanked the door open and let the monster in. Timmy let out his breath—it wasn't a monster at all. It was a brown deer with thick shoulder pads and camouflaged armor. The horns on top of his head weren't horns, either; they were antlers. The deer was quite tall, taller than any of the bears and, if you included his antlers, he was almost as tall as Timmy.

"You're awake," he said. His voice was deep and smooth and reminded Timmy a lot of his dad. "Hello, Timmy. My name is Stag, and I am the leader of the Forest Guard."

"I remember you," Timmy said. He couldn't believe he had forgotten about the large stuffed deer that his father had given him. He was younger at the time, and smaller, too; back then, the stuffed deer had been bigger than he was. "What were you doing out there in the fog?"

"We had to see if it was safe or not," Stag told him. Timmy didn't say it, but he thought that Stag must have been very brave to go out into that black fog without knowing if it would harm him or not.

The tall brown deer turned to Mother and said, "It seems to be harmless, but it's completely surrounding the cabin. I can't tell how far it stretches… it may even cover the entire forest. This is clearly the work of the Dark."

"That means we're not safe here," Mother replied. "We should move."

"Now?" said Blue. "In the middle of the night?"

"I should warn you that there's a high probability of us losing each other out there," Lucky chimed in.

Mother shook her head. "I don't know what this fog is either, but there's only one way in or out of this cabin and we can't get trapped again like we did in the barn. Maybe it's not dangerous now, but I have no doubt that it will be soon. I say we move."

"I'm with her," Bruiser said. He pounded one of his small fists against his other palm. "I'd rather fight through whatever's out there than sit here and wait to be attacked."

"What about Sly and Nimble?" asked Pilfer. "They're still out there somewhere."

"They'll be okay," said Stag. "Sly will see any danger coming, and Nimble can get up in the trees, away from this fog."

"I think we should wait for them," Lucky said quietly, "but you're our leader, Stag. Whatever you decide, we'll do."

Stag was silent for a long moment, and then he nodded once to Mother. "We move towards the river. With any luck, this fog won't stretch far, but we'll have to be careful not to lose each other."

"We could use the buddy system," Timmy suggested.

"What's that?" Sneak asked.

"It means we each pick a partner, and we keep an eye on them and make sure they don't get lost," Timmy explained. "If everyone is watching out for someone else, we won't lose anyone."

"That's a good idea," Stag agreed. "Wake the other children, and everybody choose a partner.

Pilfer, you gather up whatever food, water and supplies you can. We move in ten minutes."

CHAPTER 7:

FOG BUDDIES

Stag went first. Timmy was right; the brown-armored deer was indeed very brave. He stood tall and unafraid as he walked out of the cabin and took the first step into the fog. His fog buddy (that's what Glen called it, a "fog buddy") was Lucky, and the little yellow rabbit hopped along after him.

After Timmy had woken Glen and Anna, they

all paired off and packed the black satchel with food and water and the flashlight and the camp stove. Anna volunteered to carry the bag. And then, to Timmy's surprise, Glen had volunteered to be Timmy's fog buddy. Given his choice, he probably would have picked Mother or Anna, but he was glad that Glen offered to be his buddy and he didn't want to say no. That would have been rude.

Glen was particularly impressed by the tall brown deer. He told Timmy about how he and his dad would often see deer roaming in the field behind their barn. His dad would count the prongs on their antlers and say things like, "There's a six-pointer," or, "Look! That's an eight-pointer over there!"

"That's a ten-pointer," Glen whispered to Timmy as they watched Stag step out into the fog.

"His name is Stag," Timmy whispered back.

"Stag. That's cool." Glen was still fairly new to the Dark Corps and just seemed really glad to be a part of the adventure.

Stag and Lucky went first, and they were followed by Patch and Pilfer, and then Anna and Sneak, and then Glen and Timmy, and bringing up the rear was the trio of Bruiser, Blue, and Mother. They left the cabin in a single-file line, staying quiet (just in case there really were any Dark lurking nearby) but just a few feet from the cabin, Timmy paused.

"What is it?" Glen asked.

Timmy didn't want to say it out loud, but if he took one more step, he would be in the fog. It wasn't like any fog he had ever seen; it was thick and black and oily and almost looked like he was about to step into a giant black mud puddle. And if he was being honest with himself, he was afraid of it.

Luckily, Timmy didn't have to say it out loud, because Glen understood. "Hey, it's no big deal," he said. "Stag said it was safe, right? Look, I'll go first." He took a step forward, into the fog. It was so thick that Timmy couldn't see anything below Glen's knees; it was like his lower legs and feet just vanished. "See? Nothing to it."

Timmy nodded, gulped, and then he stepped forward too. With that one single step, he was in the fog…

And Glen was right. Nothing bad happened. He wasn't sure what he had expected to happen, but he was very glad that "nothing" was the right answer. The black fog was chilly and a bit damp, as fog tends to be, but nothing tried to grab him or pull him down into the darkness.

Bear Company, on the other hand, didn't have such an easy time. The bears were only two feet tall, so the thick fog came up past their waists and midway up their bellies. Poor Lucky, who was the smallest of the bunch, barely had his yellow head and tall rabbit ears above the darkness.

"Step carefully," Stag told them. "We won't be able to see any rocks or roots, so try not to trip." Then he did a very curious thing: he tilted his head back, opened his mouth, and made a noise that sounded exactly like the hoot of a great horned owl.

"What on earth was that?" Anna asked.

"Since our radios don't work in the forest," Lucky explained, "we use bird calls to communicate with each other. If Sly or Nimble are nearby, they'll hear the owl hoot and they'll know that means we're moving towards the river."

"I see," Anna said. "But… what happens if a

real owl hoots?"

"Hmm," said Pilfer. "That would be confusing. I guess we didn't fully think that through."

"There's only a 19.3 percent chance of an owl hooting in these woods at any given time," Lucky explained, "and only a 2.1 percent chance that an owl would hoot at the same time that we hooted, which would actually be just fine, since the message would still be—"

Stag held up a hand, the signal for the others to be quiet for a moment. Lucky fell silent. A few seconds later, a distant owl hoot echoed through the trees.

"That's Sly," said Stag. "She's not too far. I'm sure she'll meet with us along the way." The great ten-point deer led the way, stepping slowly and carefully to avoid tripping on all the things they couldn't see on the forest floor.

"This isn't so bad," Glen said, trying to sound cheerful. "Hey, watch this." He reached down and swiped at the dark fog with his fingers. Thin wisps of fog curled up into the air, and then slowly floated back down.

"No fooling around," Mother said behind them. "We still don't know what this is."

"Oh, it's not dangerous," said Bruiser. "If this was the Dark, it would have swallowed us all up by now!"

"You might be right," Mother replied, "but until we know where it came from, let's not mess with anything. Okay?"

Bruiser let out a short laugh. "You know, there is such a thing as being too careful, Mother. This is just plain ol' fog! It only *looks* dark because it's nighttime. Watch, I'll prove it to you." He aimed his right wrist at the ground—the wrist that his flasher was on.

"Bruiser, don't…!" Mother started to say, but it was too late. Bruiser fired off a quick burst of small blue balls of light—*thoom-thoom-thoom!*—right into the darkness below him. The fog evaporated instantly, forming a perfectly round hole where the balls of light hit it. For about a half-second, they could see the forest floor. Then, just as quickly, the fog closed around the hole.

"Huh," said Bruiser. "That was weird…"

Mother turned to him angrily and stuck her finger in his face. "Bruiser, if you take one more step out of line, I will leave you behind in this forest! Do you understand me?"

Bruiser was quiet for a long while, staring down at the ground.

"Well?" Mother demanded.

"Yes," Bruiser mumbled.

"Yes what?"

"Yes, I understand," said the green bear.

"Good. Now let's go—and no more shooting the fog!" Mother turned and continued along, with Bruiser trailing a bit behind.

For a whole minute, no one said anything. Then Sneak, who was in front of Timmy and Glen, snorted and said, "Ha! You got in trouble again."

CHAPTER 8:

PINS AND NEEDLES

Dark Cloud spent the entire miserable day crammed into the hollow of the old, dead oak tree. He had no idea how long a day was, and even if he did, it wouldn't have done him any good because he couldn't tell time (and even if he could, it wouldn't have done him any good, because the Dark don't wear watches).

Finally, the sun began to go down and the

sky turned from its horrible light blue to dark blue and then black. Once it was safe to come out of the tree, Dark Cloud swept out and spread his gaseous shadow as wide as he was able. If you've ever spent several hours in a car or on an airplane, and then got out to stretch your legs and walk around, you probably understand just how good it felt for the Dark to leave the tree.

If there had been anyone around to see him (which there wasn't) they would have been very frightened by what they saw. Dark Cloud's chemical-canister head with its painted white skull face floated on a tendril of black shadow, drifting along atop the mass of dark fog like a tin can on a lake.

He decided to test his strength by trying to bond with a smooth, round stone. He wrapped his fog around it, completely engulfing the rock, but he couldn't bond. He was still too weak.

If he wanted to get stronger, he would need to find other Dark, some smaller minions that he could absorb. He concentrated very hard and focused on the distant parts of his foggy body, but he could not feel any other Dark around in the forest.

But wait—there may not have been any Dark, but there *was* something. An odd feeling in a far-off part of the fog… someone was walking through his shadow. He concentrated harder. It wasn't just one someone… it was several someones.

The bears, he thought viciously. *And the boy. It must be!*

But what could he do? He did not have the strength to fight them. The small part of his shadow that was still solid would easily be destroyed by the bears and their light weapons.

Hmm, Dark Cloud thought. *Maybe I don't*

have to fight them… there could be another way.
You see, most of the Dark were quite dumb, on account of there not being schools in the dark, shadowy world they came from. But Dark Cloud was one of the few Dark that was not very dumb at all—in fact, he was pretty resourceful, which, if you recall from earlier, means clever and creative. And he had another idea of what he could do to the bears and the boy.

Suddenly he felt a very odd sensation, a feeling that he had never felt before. It was not pain, but it wasn't a tickle, either. It was a sort of uncomfortable prickling feeling that was halfway between pain and not-pain. Someone like you or I would call this feeling "pins and needles," but of course, the Dark didn't have a term for it.

He focused again, concentrating very hard on the strange sensation. Ah—that's what that was. One of the bears had shot into the fog with its light weapon. And somehow, it didn't hurt. It just felt strange. His shadow was so gaseous by now and spread so thin that he barely felt the light.

Dark Cloud laughed, hissing green gas from his canister head. He wasn't strong enough to fight the bears... but if he was careful and clever, they wouldn't be able to fight him either. He reached out again with his shadow and concentrated. It was nighttime now, and fresh fog was settling on the forest. Dark Cloud spread into it, bonding with more of the fine mist and gaining size. If he had to, he would keep absorbing fog until he covered the entire forest.

There would be no escape for the boy and his bears this time.

* * *

Nimble, the small silver squirrel with the lavender-colored eyes, clung to a very thin branch high up in a tree. She knew she should have gone back to the safe house hours ago. She definitely should have hurried back when she heard the hoot of the great horned owl, which meant that the Forest Guard was moving towards the river. But there were two very strange things going on, and Nimble was keen to investigate—which is a fancy term that means she wanted to find out just what in the world was going on.

The first strange thing, of course, was the thick black fog that covered the forest floor. Squirrels have excellent eyesight, and Nimble's was even better because she had night vision in her helmet. However, she couldn't see through the fog at all; it was as if there had been a massive oil spill all over the forest.

She was certain that it had something to do

with the tree she saw earlier, the hollow oak with the black fog rolling around it. She was also certain that it had something to do with the Dark.

And, unfortunately, she was *also* certain that the fog was growing. She would be safe up in the trees—she was called Nimble because she was quite nimble, and could leap from tree to tree gracefully and quickly—but the others would have a hard time getting anywhere in this fog.

And as I mentioned, there was not one, but two strange things that Nimble wanted to investigate. The second strange thing was a human woman, traveling alone through the forest with nothing but a flashlight and a bad attitude. Nimble had spotted her some time ago (it was very easy for Nimble to spot humans, big and clumsy and loud as they were) and had been following her ever since.

This woman did not look like the hunters

and hikers that the Forest Guard sometimes saw in the woods. She wore a black blazer and a crisp white shirt, and her hair was in a very tight bun on the top of the head. This woman was definitely not very happy; she grumbled and complained to herself as she made her way through the forest, saying things like, "When I get my hands on that boy, oh, we'll see…" and "these stupid woods better not ruin my shoes!"

Nimble followed the woman, staying high in the trees and silently jumping from branch to branch as the woman below crashed through the forest, apparently not concerned with making too much noise.

Nimble knew that her mission, as a member of the Dark Corps, was to get Timmy to his dad. But part of that mission was also keeping Timmy safe, so Nimble continued to follow the woman—because the small silver squirrel was certain that "the boy" she kept grumbling about was Timmy.

CHAPTER 9:

MARCO POLO

"**U**m… guys?" said Lucky as the five sets of fog buddies carefully made their way further through the woods towards the river. "You know I don't like to complain, but… there's a 100 percent chance that I can't see."

Timmy thought it looked like the dark fog was getting higher, but now he knew it for sure: it had risen high enough that poor Lucky was little more than a pair of yellow rabbit ears sticking up out of the darkness.

"Climb up onto my back," Stag told him. "We have to move faster," he said to the others. "This fog is definitely getting thicker."

"If we move faster, we might trip and fall," said Mother. The fog had reached her neck, so all Timmy could see was her shiny red head and glowing eyes. "And if anyone falls, we might never find them again in this mess."

"Whose idea was this, going out in the fog?" Bruiser grumbled. "I'm sure I voted to stay back in the cabin."

"What about the trees?" Anna said. "We could climb up and be safe from this fog."

"And then what?" asked Sneak. "Wait until morning? What if the fog keeps rising? What if the Dark comes? We would have nowhere to run."

"We don't have anywhere to run now!" said Patch. "We have to do something… eep!" That last part, the "eep," was a small squeak of terror, because before Patch could finish her sentence, the fog rose once more, and then all five members of Bear Company vanished from view, along with Pilfer the raccoon.

"Mother?" Timmy said. "Mother, where'd you go?!" The fog was almost up to his chest now, and rising quickly.

"I'm here!" Her voice floated to him as clearly as if she'd been standing right next to him, but the fog was so thick that it was very difficult to tell which direction it came from.

"No one move," Stag ordered. "Stay right where you are, and we'll find you."

"I wish Sly was here," said Lucky, perched on one of Stag's thick shoulder pads.

Something brushed against Timmy's leg.

It was probably one of the bears, and Timmy certainly didn't mean to jump in fright, but jumping in fright is a natural reaction when something that you can't see touches you. It's a lot like being in the ocean and feeling something rub against you—it's probably just a curious little fish, but we're often afraid of what we can't see.

Timmy jumped in fright, and his foot caught on a root. He fell backwards into the fog. Suddenly the entire world vanished from sight— there was nothing but blackness all around him, the thickest, darkest darkness he had ever seen. It was like being inside of a shadow (or, in this case, it very much *was* being inside of a shadow). The fog felt damp and cold and it clung to his cheeks. For a few seconds he just sat there, on his rear on the mossy forest floor, unable to move or see or do much of anything other than breathe and be afraid. There were voices all around him, the confused and frightened voices of the bears and the Forest Guard trying to find each other, but he wasn't paying any attention to their words.

Then, a hand touched his arm. He quickly pulled it away.

"Hey," said Glen's voice, "it's me. Are you okay?"

"Yeah," said Timmy, "I think so." He felt Glen's hand again, touching his left shoulder.

"I'm going to hang onto you," said Glen, "so we don't lose each other."

"Good idea." Timmy stood up slowly. He was expecting, any second, to rise above the fog, but even standing at full height and on his tiptoes, all he saw was black.

The fog was high and thick, and now over his head. They were trapped in the darkness.

"What do we do?" he asked in a whisper. His voice sounded very small.

"I have another idea," Glen said. Then he called out, "Marco!"

At first there was no answer. But then Anna's voice floated to them: "Polo!"

"Marco!" Glen shouted again.

"Polo!" Anna called back.

"Polo!" Blue shouted from somewhere.

"Polo!" said Pilfer.

"Oh, this is useless!" Glen groaned. "I can't tell which direction they're coming from!" Some of the voices sounded more distant than others, but the fog was too thick to tell where anyone was.

"Everyone, hang onto your fog buddy!" said Stag. His voice was clear, but it did not sound close. "Find the nearest tree, and climb until you're out of the fog!"

Timmy put both his hands out in front of him and took a small step forward. He nearly fell again, this time on a rock, but he steadied himself. With Glen's hand on his shoulder, he took tiny steps, being careful to lift his feet up high to avoid tripping.

He counted his footsteps so they would have some idea of how far they had gone. He counted to fifteen, and then twenty, and then twenty-five, and they still hadn't found a tree.

"We're going too far," said Glen. "We'll lose the others!"

"How hard can it be to find a tree in a forest?" Timmy whispered back. "It's like they all disappeared!" If Timmy and Glen had been able to see where they were going, they would have known that they had stumbled into a small clearing, and that it would be another twenty-five steps before they found a tree again.

"Wait," said Glen over his shoulder. "Listen."

Timmy stopped and held his breath. "I don't

hear anything," he said.

"Exactly. I don't hear anything either. We went too far, Timmy. We're lost!"

"Marco!" said Timmy. "Marco! Marco?"

"*Polo*," hissed a soft voice.

A chill of terror ran up Timmy's spine. Glen gripped his shoulder even harder. They couldn't tell where it was coming from, but the voice was very, very close.

CHAPTER 10:

AN AUSTRALIAN CRESTED PIGEON

Neither of the boys moved a muscle. They were frozen in fear. The hissing voice had made their blood run cold, which is a phrase that means they were so scared the Dark had found them that a cold feeling ran through their whole bodies.

"Timmy." The voice came again, but this time it wasn't a hissing whisper—it was clearer, closer, and sounded female. "I'm sorry, I didn't mean to frighten you. Listen carefully: I can't see you if you're not moving. Take one step forward."

Timmy didn't say anything—he had no idea who the voice belonged to—but he did as he was asked and took one step forward.

"Good," said the voice. "Now keep moving in a straight line. You'll reach a tree in another twenty-four steps."

"Who are you?" Timmy asked. "Where did the others go?"

"My name is Sly," the voice said. "I don't know where the others are. I found you first. You must have gotten separated quickly; I think everyone panicked and went in different directions. Now, twenty-four steps forward, if you please."

Timmy stepped carefully, and in a short time

he and Glen reached the opposite end of the clearing and his hands brushed the rough bark of a tree. "Now what?" he asked.

"Reach up."

He did, and his hands found a low branch. He pulled himself up, and then reached up again until he found another branch. Glen climbed up after him.

"Good," said the voice. "A little further…"

Timmy climbed up one more branch, and suddenly he could see again. Even though it was still nighttime and the moonlight was dim through the leaves, it was as wonderful as a sunrise to be able to see anything at all—especially the red and pink fox that sat on the branch next to him.

There were a hundred questions in his mind, like "where did the others go?" and "how did you find us through the fog?" but the question that he blurted out was, "Do foxes climb trees?"

"Foxes are excellent climbers," said Sly. "And great jumpers, too."

"Can you see through the fog?" Glen asked as he pulled himself up onto the branch.

"No," Sly answered, "Timmy's dad built me with motion sensors, so I can see things that are moving, even in this fog. I could see you two as you were walking, but I can't see the trees and rocks and roots."

"So… I guess that means no one can ever sneak up on you," said Glen.

"That's right. That's why they call me Sly— everyone thinks I must be very cunning, but really I just always see them coming."

"Can you see the others?" Timmy asked hopefully.

Sly shook her head sadly. "No, I can't. The range of my motion sensors is only about fifty feet. I can tell you that there's an adorable family of chipmunks living about twenty-three feet to the east, but none of the others are nearby."

Timmy sighed. "What do we do now?"

"Well, there's only one thing we can do," Sly said. She opened her mouth wide and let out two sharp squawks that sounded very much like a parakeet. Then she waited and listened, and a moment later, from somewhere in the distant black fog, came the distinct call of a whooping crane.

"What do those bird calls mean?" Glen asked.

"Well, I tweeted that I found you and that you were safe," Sly explained. "And Stag whooped back that we should go on to the river ourselves, and that they'll try to find their way as best they can."

"We're not actually going to go without them, are we?" Timmy didn't like the idea of moving on without the bears, and he really didn't like the idea of going back down into the fog.

"Of course not," said Sly with a wink. "Stag won't like that we disobeyed his order, but I'm the only one that can find them in this fog. You two must stay here—don't leave this tree, okay? I won't go far. And if you hear the call of an Australian crested pigeon, wave your arms in the air so that I can see you with my motion sensors and find my way back." With that, Sly jumped off the branch. She was right; foxes were very excellent jumpers. A second later, she disappeared into the black fog below.

"Don't worry," said Glen. "She'll find the others, I'm sure."

"Definitely," said Timmy, trying to sound more certain than he really was.

"Hey... do you have any idea what an Australian crested pigeon sounds like?" Glen asked.

"Nope," Timmy said. "Not a clue."

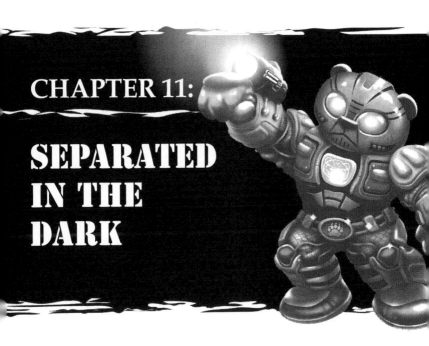

CHAPTER 11:

SEPARATED IN THE DARK

"**S**tupid fog," Bruiser grumbled. "Stupid Dark. Stupid nighttime. Stupid plan to go out into the stupid fog at stupid nighttime."

He couldn't see a thing. He tried to find the other bears by their glowing eyes, but the fog was so thick and dark that it swallowed the light. He tried shouting "Marco!" a few times, but there was no answer. He had lost his fog buddies,

Mother and Blue, and all the others too. Bruiser wandered about, occasionally stumbling a little on a branch or stone, his hands out in front of him so that he didn't run headfirst into any trees.

He tried climbing one, shimmying up the trunk until he could reach the branches. He made his way above the fog and into the moonlight, but there was no one else around. None of the others had climbed trees—or if they did, they weren't anywhere near him. He sat there in the tree for a little while, but soon he got very bored. Bruiser wasn't the kind of bear that waited around, so back down into the fog he went.

"Stupid fog," he grumbled again.

* * *

Anna held Sneak's hand as they sat together on the forest floor, in the utter darkness. They hadn't moved at all since they were separated from the others, but somehow no one had found them.

"Maybe we should move," said Anna quietly. "I don't think the others are around here anymore."

"I don't think that's a good idea," Sneak replied. "Stag said we should stay put. Someone will find us. I'm sure of it."

"But what if the thing that finds us isn't what we want to find us?" Anna asked. She was not afraid of the dark, but she was a little afraid of the Dark—and she was definitely afraid of the Dark in the dark, because they would never see the shadows coming.

Sneak squeezed her hand. "Hey, don't worry. There's no better bear for you to be with. Not only am I the sneakiest, but I'm also the bravest, *and* the fiercest."

"Oh, really?" Anna smiled. "I thought Bruiser was the fiercest."

"Ha! He wishes that was true. If anything, Bruiser's just the biggest complainer... *Heek!*" Sneak let out a half-hiccup, half-sneeze. "Sorry. I can't help that. It's a malfunction in my hardware."

"Sneak?" said a voice from the darkness. "Was that you?"

"Hey," said Anna as she stood up excitedly. "I think that's Patch! Yes, we're over here!"

"I can't tell where 'here' is," Patch called back. "How do we find you?"

Anna thought for a moment. "Oh, I know! Patch, find a rock and toss it."

"Um, okay... I got one." Patch threw the rock, and Anna listened for the thud. It sounded far away.

"Okay, now turn around and throw another

rock in the opposite direction," she told Patch. She waited to hear the thud—and this time, it sounded much closer. "Great! Now start walking in a straight line that way."

They repeated that process, Patch tossing a rock and then taking a few steps in the right direction and then throwing another rock, until Anna could reach out and touch the yellow bear's smooth armored head. She knelt down and hugged Patch tightly.

"Is anyone with you?" she asked.

"I'm here," said Pilfer. "I didn't lose my fog buddy."

"At least there are four of us together now," said Sneak. "Let's go find the others."

* * *

Every once in a while, you might meet

someone who is so incredibly unhappy that you may say to yourself, "Boy, that is the unhappiest person I've ever seen! I don't know how anyone could be any unhappier than *that*."

If you've ever said that, it means that you've never met Ms. Gertrude—because at that very moment, stumbling around in the darkness of the forest, Ms. Gertrude was about the unhappiest she had ever been in her whole life. The strange, thick fog that had been up to her knees before had risen, higher and higher, until it was over her head. She couldn't see a thing, and she grumbled very loudly about it.

She was certain that her flashlight was working just fine, and that the batteries were fresh, but she still couldn't see anything. She clicked the button on and off, but there was no light; it was as if the black fog swallowed it up. And, of course, she grumbled about that.

She was very sure that her shiny, black shoes were completely ruined in this filthy forest, even though she couldn't see them. And she grumbled about that.

As if all that wasn't bad enough, Ms. Gertrude ran right into a tree. She bumped her head and grumbled, and then she grumbled again because she was very sure that her crisp white shirt was now ruined too.

In the highest branches over Ms. Gertrude's head, safe from the fog, Nimble followed the sound of the grumbling as best she could. It was hard to tell where it was coming from, but as long as it sounded close, Nimble knew she wasn't very far from the strange, clumsy woman. The little silver squirrel was determined to keep her from finding Timmy.

And then, a curious thing happened: Nimble looked down, and she could see the woman's head. Then she could see her shoulders, and her arms, and the yellow beam of light from her flashlight.

Ms. Gertrude looked just as surprised as Nimble, glancing all around in the moonlight. "Well!" said Ms. Gertrude indignantly (which means "annoyed at being treated unfairly"). "At least something decent has happened in these woods!"

The fog was lowering. While this was good news for Ms. Gertrude, because it was now lower than waist-high and she could see again, this was bad news for Nimble—because it meant this woman would be able to see Timmy if she found him.

* * *

The first part of Dark Cloud's clever plan

had worked perfectly. He had absorbed quite a lot of fog now—he was sure that he was now the biggest Dark that had ever lived, even larger than the legendary Dark named Brobdingnag, who was said to have had a shadow so enormous that his head touched the sky.

The first part of Dark Cloud's clever plan, the part that had worked perfectly, was to gather his fog thickly around the bears so that they could not see. In their confusion and panic they had separated from each other. Next, Dark Cloud spread his foggy body out as wide as he could. He covered the entire forest floor with fog, so that there was no escape for the bears and the boy.

He concentrated hard, feeling around the forest with his wide shadow. He could tell that they had separated into smaller groups. There was a group of four, two groups of two, and a few others by themselves. He thought that he should go after the ones that were alone, but he doubted the boy was wandering about the forest without at least one of the bears. They were his protectors, that much was clear. The group of four had a human with them, he could tell. That's where he would go.

You see, the Dark had trouble telling one human from another. The whole reason that Anna had first joined Bear Company on their journey was because some of the Dark thought that Anna might have been Timmy and attacked her, and the bears had saved her. So even though Dark Cloud could tell that there was a human child and three others together in the forest, he could not tell that the human child was Anna, as you already know. He also could not feel Timmy anywhere in his fog, since Timmy was safely up in a tree with Glen at the same moment.

All Dark Cloud knew for sure was that there was a child in the fog and quite near to where his chemical-canister head and shadowy tendrils currently were, and so he stalked off silently in that direction.

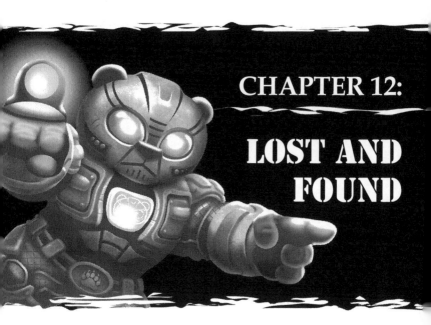

CHAPTER 12:

LOST AND FOUND

Even though Sly could see movement in the thick black fog, she could not see anything that was staying still, which meant that she still had to move quite slowly in the black fog to avoid running into trees or tripping over rocks. She counted her steps as she moved, being careful not to go too far from the tree where she had left Timmy and Glen; after all, her motion sensors only worked for a range of about fifty feet, which isn't very far at all, and if she lost the tree she would lose the boys.

Sly counted carefully to fifty, making sure that she did not skip any numbers, and then she stopped. If she took one more step forward, she might not be able to find her way back. She looked left and right but couldn't see any motion at all, other than the occasional small woodland critter.

"Marco," she called out quietly. "Anyone out there?"

There was no answer. She tried a bird call—specifically, she squawked out the greeting call of the Tasmanian emu, which was the Forest Guard's code for "hello, I'm close by, where are you?" But there was no call back.

Just as Sly was beginning to lose any hope of finding the others, a wondrous thing happened—

she could see the moonlight, even if just a little bit. At first she thought it was her eyes playing tricks on her in the darkness, but little by little, she could see the trees, and the leaves above, and her own two hands in front of her face. It was as if someone was lifting a veil from over her face. The fog was lifting. (Although, as you already know, Dark Cloud was simply spreading his fog over the entire forest.) Even so, this was a good thing for Sly, because it meant that she could find the others without worrying about losing the tree that held Timmy and Glen.

She hesitated, which is a word that means she paused because she was uncertain. If she continued on to find the others, Timmy and Glen would be left alone. But then again, they were safe up in the tree. Yes, she decided, the right choice was to find Stag and Lucky and Pilfer and get Timmy to the river together. She continued onwards to find her friends.

* * *

"Hey, Timmy. Look." Glen sat on the branch up in the wide tree and pointed downward. "It looks like the fog is getting lower."

Timmy squinted down at the ground. All he saw was blackness, but Glen seemed to be right; it did look like it was lower than before. He hoped that Sly would have an easier time finding the others now.

"I'm going to check it out." Glen climbed down to the next lowest branch.

"I don't think that's a good idea," Timmy said. "Sly said to stay up here…"

"I'll come right back." Glen was already halfway to the ground. "I just want to see." He hopped down from the last branch and landed on the forest floor. "Ha! I was right. Look." The dark, murky fog didn't even come up to Glen's waist. "This is great! Once Sly finds the others, we'll be able to get to the river, no problem!"

"I knew it!" said a very sharp, crisp voice behind him. Glen turned around quickly and found himself blinded by a very bright yellow light, shining directly in his eyes. "I knew I would find you in these woods, Timothy Barnes!"

Glen put one hand up to shield his eyes from the harsh flashlight. "I'm not Timmy," he said. "My name is Glen."

"Hmm," said the voice. "You're right. You're *not* Timothy Barnes. But you were talking to someone just now. Who was it?"

Up in the branches, Timmy stayed perfectly still and perfectly silent. He couldn't see the person that was holding the flashlight, but he knew that voice. It was the same voice that had sharply said "lights out!" every night at bedtime for the last month or so.

"I was talking to myself," Glen said bravely.

"I don't believe you." Ms. Gertrude lowered the flashlight and stared into the boy's face. "And I don't believe that you're alone in these woods, either. Someone else is nearby, and you're going to tell me who and where they are."

"Nuh-uh," said Glen.

Ms. Gertrude grabbed him by the arm. "I don't know exactly what's going on here, boy, but I do know that my shoes are ruined and my shirt is a mess and I'm very unhappy. So you *will* tell me where Timothy Barnes is, or I will make you very unhappy too!"

"Ow!" Glen shouted. "Trim your fingernails, lady!"

Up in the tree, Timmy didn't dare to breathe. How had Ms. Gertrude followed him all this way? *Why* had Ms. Gertrude followed him all this way? She hadn't been a very good nanny, and she didn't seem to care for children very much. What was she doing in the forest, looking for him?

Suddenly, something landed on the branch right next to him without making a sound. Timmy almost gasped out loud, but the small silver squirrel with the lavender eyes put a finger against her lips, as if to say, "Shhh."

Down on the ground, Ms. Gertrude held onto Glen's arm and half-dragged him away from the tree. "Come on," she commanded. "Whoever you were talking to can't be far away, and I'd bet a new pair of shoes that it was Timothy Barnes!"

"I don't know what you're talking about!" said Glen. "I don't even know anyone named Timothy! I've never met a Timothy! Is Timothy even a real name?" But Ms. Gertrude wasn't listening. She was looking for him.

Lucky for Timmy, she wasn't looking up.

"We have to go after them!" he whispered to the small silver squirrel.

"No," said Nimble. "I'm sorry, but that woman isn't the Dark, and she didn't find you. We should stay here and wait for the others."

"But Glen is my friend! I can't let anything happen to him," Timmy said.

The silver squirrel sighed. "Okay, how about this? I'll go and get Glen back. You stay and wait for the others."

"Okay," said Timmy.

"Promise?" said the squirrel.

"Promise." Timmy crossed his fingers behind his back.

"See you at the river." Nimble jumped from the branch and soared through the air for a moment, flattening her great bushy tail before landing without a sound on the branch of a neighboring tree. In two seconds she was out of sight.

Timmy really, really hated lying, and he really didn't like to break promises—but he did cross his fingers. Glen was not just his friend, but also his fog buddy. He couldn't lose him. And almost as important as that, Timmy really wanted to know how and why Ms. Gertrude was looking for him in the forest. As soon as Nimble was out of sight, he climbed down from the tree and followed them. He could see the sweeping yellow beam of Ms. Gertrude's flashlight up ahead, moving back and forth slowly as she looked for him.

He would just have to make sure to stay hidden.

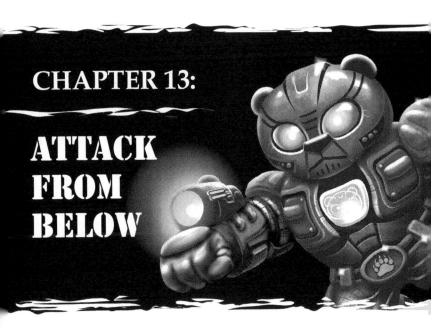

CHAPTER 13:

ATTACK FROM BELOW

Dark Cloud swept quickly towards the group of four. He kept his chemical-canister head low in the fog. Though the bears and humans couldn't see where they were going in the dark black mist, the Dark could see just fine; he was used to the shadows and darkness.

The four of them—Anna, Sneak, Patch, and Pilfer—were making their way slowly through the forest, trying to find the others. The fog had just recently seemed to recede enough that they could see again, and Sneak was right in the middle of telling everyone how happy he was to see anything at all.

It should be a piece of cake finding the others now," he was saying. "I bet any moment now we'll see some glowing eyes between the trees, and it'll be Mother and Blue, or Stag and Lucky, or…"

Anna stopped and looked to her left. She blinked in surprise. One moment, Sneak had been walking alongside her. In the next moment, he was simply gone.

"Sneak?" she said. "Sneak! Where'd you go?"

Dark Cloud wrapped his shadowy tendril around the orange bear's leg and yanked him under the fog so quickly that he didn't even have time to cry out. Sneak could see nothing but blackness as he was dragged over moss and dirt and rocks, away from the others. He aimed his flasher and tried to shoot whatever had a hold on him, but it was no use. The small balls of light hit nothing but fog.

Dark Cloud slithered over the bear's body. This was his moment. He was finally going to bond with one of the bears, take control of their light weapon, and then he would be the most powerful of all the Dark. His tendrils reached out and over the orange bear, completely covering him, ready to bond with—

"Hey," said Sneak. "Stop! That tickles."

Something was wrong. Dark Cloud could not bond with the bear… he was still too weak. *How foolish of me!* he thought angrily. He hadn't even been able to bond with a rock earlier. There was no way he was strong enough to bond with the bear.

The little orange bear twisted and fought against him, trying to stand again. Dark Cloud lifted his chemical head and hissed a green breath of gas in the bear's face. Sneak was suddenly very dizzy, swaying back and forth.

"Oooh…" he mumbled. "That's some… really… bad… breath." The orange bear toppled over.

A short distance away, Anna searched the fog desperately for Sneak. "Wait!" she called to the other two. "Sneak disappeared!"

"Flashers up!" said Pilfer. He and Patch pointed the weapons on their wrist at… Well, they didn't really know where to point them. The fog was everywhere. And if the Dark were in the fog, there was no way to see them coming.

"Okay," said Patch slowly. "I think the best thing for us to do is to—*gah!*" In a half a second, the yellow bear was sucked down into the fog.

"Patch!" Anna shouted.

"Don't panic!" said Pilfer. "We need to stay calm. Let's get to a tree and—*whoa!*" The raccoon disappeared in an instant.

Anna stood perfectly still, holding her breath so that there was no other sound. She wanted to hear someone's voice, to know that they were okay... but she heard nothing.

She was alone.

Then, something rose from the fog. If Lucky had been there, the little yellow rabbit probably would have told her that there was a 75.6 percent chance that it was one of her friends. But Lucky wasn't there, and it wasn't one of her friends.

A strange cylindrical head rose up from the fog. It had a white painted skull on it and hissed a green gas with every breath. The canister sat atop a thin tendril of shadow, so that it looked like a large head on a very thin body—which might have been kind of funny-looking, except that this was no time for laughter.

"*Are you afraid of the Dark?*" the skull hissed.

Anna remembered this Dark. It was the one that Bear Company fought in the field, the one that had injured Bruiser. And yes, she was quite afraid at the moment. She couldn't help the trembling in her arms and legs. She was alone, in a fog, with the Dark, and without her friends.

But as I've mentioned before, Anna was also very brave. So she stood up tall and lifted her chin and said, "No. I'm not afraid of you."

"*You are afraid,*" said Dark Cloud. "*I can smell it...*" The Dark paused, and then said. "*Wait. You're not the boy.*"

Anna groaned. "Of course not! I don't know how many times I have to explain it to you strange things. I'm a girl!"

Dark Cloud hissed. He had made a mistake and chosen the wrong child. This girl didn't matter to him; it was the boy he was after.

Then, in the next few seconds, several things happened almost all at once. First there was a sound—*whiiiirrr*—and both Anna and Dark Cloud turned to see what it was.

Then there was another sound, a much louder one—*THOOM!* And a beam of blue light cut into Dark Cloud like a hot knife through butter (which is a saying that means "very, very easily").

The shadow hissed and immediately dropped back down into the fog, disappearing from sight. Anna looked left and right to see who had shot the flasher beam.

"Are you alright?" asked the fox. It was red and pink and its eyes glowed in the darkness.

"Yes, I think so," said Anna. "You must be Sly. Or is it Nimble?"

"I'm Sly," said the fox. "But I'm afraid we don't have much time for greetings and get-to-know-yous. That was a Dark, and where there's one, there's always more. Were you alone?"

"No," Anna told her. "I was with Sneak and Patch and Pilfer, but I don't know where they've gone."

"Here," said Sneak. His voice sounded weak and woozy, like he had just woken up from a very long nap. "I'm over here."

"The other two must be nearby," said Sly. "I'll find them. You two, get up a tree, and hurry! There's no time to waste."

Anna ran to Sneak and helped the little orange bear up the nearest tree, and then she climbed up next to him. The fox, Sly, was somehow able to find Pilfer and Patch in the fog very quickly (of course, Anna did not know about Sly's motion sensors, and Pilfer and Patch were just waking up too). Sly helped the bear and the raccoon into the tree, and then with one excellent leap, she joined them on a thick branch.

"Now what do we do?" Anna asked. "And what about the others?"

"For now, we wait," said Sly. "If we're sure the coast is clear, we'll keep moving. But if it's not… then I'm afraid the others will have to find their own way."

* * *

From nearby, Dark Cloud hissed angrily as he watched the fox and bear and raccoon climb up the tree. He had been careless, thinking that he could attack them so easily. And he had paid for it, too—the beam of light had weakened him even more than he already was.

At least he knew that these five weren't going anywhere soon. He reached out with his shadow, concentrating very hard to see where the others were. There was something new now—two more humans in his forest. No… it was *three* humans, and they were close together.

One of them had to be the boy, he just knew it.

Dark Cloud swept away, using the fog to hide his shadow as he headed towards the other humans.

CHAPTER 14:

DON'T TELL ME THE ODDS

Mother was beginning to lose hope. She was alone in the fog, and even though she could see again, the only way that was helpful was to see just how alone she was. She knew that she had not gone very far from where she'd lost the others, but somehow they must have gone very far, because she couldn't see or hear anyone.

"Is anyone here?" she called out. "Marco?"

"Polo," came a voice from above her. She looked up and almost laughed.

"Blue!" she said with relief. "There you are. How did you get up in that tree?"

"When we lost the others, Stag said to climb." Blue slid down the trunk of the tree and came to a stop beside her. "So I climbed."

"Well, I'm glad *someone* listened," said Mother. Blue didn't have to ask who *someone* might be; he knew she meant Bruiser, their other fog buddy, who had clearly wandered away and was lost out there in the fog.

"I suppose we should go find him," said Blue.

"No," said Mother firmly. "I told him that if he stepped out of line one more time, I would leave him in this forest—and he very literally stepped out of line. We'll go to the river. If Timmy is with the Forest Guard or the rest of

Bear Company, that's what they would do."
Mother felt very bad saying that she would leave
Bruiser behind, but he *had* wandered off alone,
and she *had* warned him. "All we can hope is
that Bruiser makes it on his own. Otherwise, he's
staying behind."

Blue's eyes shined a little brighter as he
brought up the GPS map in his helmet. "It's still
very fuzzy," he said. "I'm barely getting any
signal… but if I had to guess, I would say the
river is that way." He pointed to the northwest,
and the two of them headed that way.

After a few minutes of walking, Blue said,
"Hey, Mother. Do you happen to know how to
hoot like an owl?"

"I've never tried it before," said Mother.
"Why do you ask?"

"Well, Stag said that the hoot meant they
were heading towards the river," said Blue.

"Maybe if we give a hoot, anyone who is close enough to hear it will know where we're going."

"Hmm. I guess I could give it a try. Okay, here goes." Mother lifted her head and opened her mouth and called out, "Hoot!"

Blue snorted, doing his best to hold in a laugh. "That wasn't an owl hoot! That was just you shouting 'hoot'!"

"Oh, be quiet!" Mother said. "I've never done this before, you know. Let me try again. Here goes… Hoot! Hoot!"

This time Blue couldn't hold it in. He giggled so hard he nearly fell over. You see, sometimes, even when you're in a bad situation and you're beginning to lose hope that things might get better, you still need to laugh—because laughing feels good, and without it, the world is a very, very dark place.

"Mother?" said a deep, strong voice from

nearby. "Is that you?" From out of the darkness came two red glowing eyes and a very tall pair of antlers. And on one of the deer's large, brown shoulder pads was a small yellow rabbit with long ears.

"Stag! Lucky!" said Mother happily. "Is Timmy with you? Or Anna, or Glen?"

"No," said Stag. "I'm afraid we haven't seen or heard them. We heard giggling and followed it here, to you."

"Sorry," said Blue, "I was laughing at Mother, trying to hoot like an owl."

"Is that was that was?" Lucky asked. "I thought an animal was grievously injured."

That caused Blue to laugh again, even harder.

"Even so," said Stag, "Mother has the right idea. We were heading to the river, so we have to assume that's where the others have gone. If we're lucky, they're together."

"I would say there's about a 3.7 chance that they're all together," said Lucky, "but hey… we can hope, right?"

"You know, Lucky," Mother grumbled as the four of them headed towards the river, "sometimes it's not so great to know the odds."

* * *

At about the same time that Mother and Blue found Stag and Lucky, someone else was nearby, though they had no way of knowing about each other. High over their heads—even higher than the highest branches and the canopy of leaves—a dark shape flew over the forest. It was almost impossible to tell what it looked like because the shadow blended against the night sky, but if you had very, very good vision, you might be able to see the black outline of a vulture.

The Dark called Fright soared over the forest. He had been to the old barn, where there had clearly been a battle. He had gone to the wide field and found the sledgehammer and scythe sitting in the grass. Now he flew over the forest, but he couldn't see a thing from up here because of the large trees and thick leaves.

But he could tell that something was not quite right.

He flew downward and through the leaves, entering the forest, and landed on a high-up branch of a tree. What he saw when he looked down was very, very strange.

"*What is this?*" Fright hissed as he examined the black fog. He had never seen anything quite like it before. He flew down once more for an even closer look, landing in it. This was certainly the work of a Dark, he knew that much. He tried to absorb just a small piece of it, to see what would happen… and right away he understood.

"*Dark Cloud!*" he squawked. "*What have you done to yourself?*"

Of course, the fog could not answer, and Dark Cloud's chemical-canister head was some distance away. Fright had to tell Total Dark about this right away. No Dark had ever stretched themselves this far. Fright wondered if he covered the whole forest…

The fog reached for him, climbing up his vulture-shadow body in thin wisps, like vines climbing up a fence. Fright quickly flew upward, out of the mist. Dark Cloud must have been very weak; the fog was instinctively reaching for him, desperate to bond with any Dark that it could ("instinctively" meaning "something you do without having to think about it," like breathing or blinking or jumping in fear when black fog tries to reach out and grab you).

Fright swooped up above the trees again, across the forest for a short distance, and then darted back down to see just how large Dark Cloud's shadow had become. It was incredible. It must have stretched for a mile, maybe more!

He took to the sky once more and pointed his sharp, knife-like beak in the direction of the secret ice base where Total Dark was hiding out. Their leader needed to know what was happening here.

CHAPTER 15:

FOUND AT LAST

"**A**re you going to drag me through this whole forest?" Glen grumbled to the strange woman with the tight bun on top of her head. She still had his arm tightly in her grip, and held a flashlight with the other as she searched for Timmy Barnes.

"Yes," she said sharply, "until you tell me where your friend is."

"I don't know where he is!" Glen shouted. It wasn't a lie; by this point, they had gone so far away from the tree where Timmy was hiding that Glen couldn't possibly hope to get back to it.

Ms. Gertrude grumbled softly under her breath. There were a million places for a little boy to hide in the woods, especially at night, and *especially* with this dense, dark fog.

"What are you doing out here all alone anyway?" Ms. Gertrude scolded. "Shouldn't you be at home with your family?"

"I lost my family," Glen said. "I'm trying to find them again."

"Oh." For a moment, the fingers that were wrapped tightly around Glen's arm loosened a little. "Well… still. The forest at nighttime is no place for little boys to be. Now, if I let you go, will you promise not to run away?"

"Yes," Glen promised. Ms. Gertrude let go of his arm, and Glen rubbed the spot where she had been squeezing it—not because it hurt, but because he wanted to make her feel bad.

"Why do you want to find Timmy so much, anyway?" he asked.

"Because," she said, "I'm his nanny. I'm responsible for him until his father comes home." That wasn't a lie, either. Ms. Gertrude didn't like children very much, but she didn't want to see anyone get hurt. All she wanted was for Timmy's dad to finish his work and come home to his son so that she could move on to another mission. But she couldn't do that if Timmy ran off to go who-knows-where. There was no way that Timmy knew his father was working in a top-secret base in the Arctic, and even if he did, there definitely wasn't any way that Timmy could get there alone.

"Is that the truth?" Glen asked. "You're his nanny? Because you don't look like any sort of nanny I've ever seen."

"Yes," Ms. Gertrude said in annoyance. "It's the truth."

Glen thought for a moment. He knew that Bear Company wanted to help Timmy find his dad, but if this woman was telling the truth, she could help, too. Maybe she could even team up with them and help get Timmy to where he needed to be.

"Okay," said Glen. "I'll help you find him." He took a deep breath and called out, "Timmy! Where are you? It's okay to come out now!"

"Well, I could have done *that*," Ms. Gertrude grumbled. "Come on, we haven't looked this way…" She took one more step in the other direction, and suddenly her left foot splashed down into cold, ankle-deep water. "Oh!" she exclaimed as she pulled her foot back. If her shoes weren't ruined before, they certainly were now.

She shined her flashlight beam ahead of her. They seemed to be standing on the bank of a wide, rushing river. The fog was still thick, but after a few feet it faded into a grayish mist and she could see the rushing water in the moonlight.

"The river," said Glen quietly. "We made it."

"What was that?" Ms. Gertrude asked.

"Uh, nothing!" Glen said quickly. "I just said that maybe we should go back. I don't think Timmy would swim across the river."

"No, you're right," she said. "Okay, let's go back the way we came, and hope to…" She turned back, and the beam of her flashlight swept right across the face of a young boy.

"*There* you are!" Ms. Gertrude almost shouted. "I've been everywhere looking for you, young man! Do you have any idea how much these shoes cost?!"

Timmy was very confused, because he had no idea why she was talking about her shoes. But that wasn't the important question at the moment. "Ms. Gertrude, why are you here? How did you find me? Are you following me?"

"I came to take you back home," she said, which only answered one of his questions. "Until your father returns, I am responsible for you. Now come along, we're going back to the city right now!"

"I'm going to see my father," said Timmy. "He needs my help. The Dark has come, and the bears are helping me get to him…"

"The Dark? The bears?" Ms. Gertrude laughed. "That's right, the talking bears. I've heard so much about them." She looked left and right, shining her flashlight beam on the trees and the rocks and the fog and the river, and then she said, "Where are these bears of yours? I don't see them anywhere."

"Well… we got separated in the fog," Timmy explained. "They said we would meet at the river. They're coming. I know they are."

Ms. Gertrude sighed. "That doesn't matter now. You're coming home with me."

"No, I'm going to find my dad."

"No," said Ms. Gertrude. She took a big step towards him. "You're coming… home… with… *ooph!*" Ms. Gertrude's foot caught against something solid—something that she couldn't see in the fog. She fell forward. The flashlight went flying out of her hand and into the darkness, the black fog swallowing the light instantly.

Ms. Gertrude didn't know it, but while she was talking to Timmy, a small, silver squirrel was hiding in the fog near her feet. You see, a squirrel's tail is useful for a great many things, but one of the best uses is to trip people. As Ms. Gertrude took a step forward, Nimble flattened her big, silver tail, and the woman sprawled forward.

"What in the world was that?" Ms. Gertrude asked as she climbed back to her feet. "It couldn't have been a rock or a root... I swear, I felt it move!"

She didn't have to wonder for very long, because as soon as she was on her feet again, Nimble popped up from beneath the fog. Ms. Gertrude suddenly found herself staring at what appeared to be a squirrel, wearing silver armor, its eyes glowing lavender, and a strange weapon on its right wrist.

"You will not take Timmy away from here," the squirrel said. "I won't let you."

If you've been paying attention—and I'm

sure you have—then by now you know that Ms. Gertrude had been certain of a great many things. But in that moment, staring at a thing that was clearly impossible, Ms. Gertrude suddenly wasn't sure of anything at all. A hundred questions formed in her brain, and all of them hurried to her mouth at the same time, causing a huge traffic jam so that all she could say was, "Uh… um… uh…"

"Ms. Gertrude," Timmy said. "This is my friend, Nimble."

Ms. Gertrude blinked at the small creature. The only thing that she could think to say at the moment was, "You're not a bear."

"No," said Nimble, "but the bears are coming."

"You think that's weird?" said Glen. "There's also a cow."

"And a pig," said Timmy.

"And an eagle…"

"And a stag…"

"And wolves…"

"Stop!" Ms. Gertrude shouted. "Please, stop! You're making my head hurt."

"Ms. Gertrude," said Timmy. "Bear Company and the Dark Corps are the good guys. It's the Dark that we have to worry about—they're the shadows, the ones that are trying to take scared children away."

"They're real too?" Ms. Gertrude asked. Her voice was very small, like a frightened child's.

"I'm afraid so," said Timmy. "But the bears have taught me that you don't have to be afraid of them. The bears fight them, with the light…"

"Hey, Timmy!" said Glen. "Look! There's one now!" He pointed behind them.

Sure enough, there was the small shape of a bear coming their way. Timmy smiled. They had made it! "Who's there?" he asked. "Is that you, Patch? Bruiser? Blue? Sneak? Mother?"

The bear said nothing as it walked towards them in the darkness. He couldn't tell what color its armor was, and he couldn't see their glowing eyes in the fog.

In fact, their eyes weren't glowing at all.

As the bear-shaped silhouette reached Timmy, he reached out and touched it. You see, it was still very dark outside, and even though there was some amount of moonlight, the fog swallowed up much of the light and made it difficult to see.

And in case you were wondering about the word in that last paragraph—"silhouette"—it means a dark outline of something (in this case, a two-foot-tall bear standing on its hind legs). So now that you know what a silhouette is, I'm sure you can guess where this is heading, and

I'm sure you feel a small ball of dread in the pit of your stomach too, just like Timmy did earlier.

Because as his fingers reached out and touched the bear, it evaporated. The bear shape was made of dark fog, and it fell away in wisps. Timmy took a step backwards, but it was too late.

From out of the low-hanging fog came a cylindrical shape—a familiar chemical canister with a white painted skull on the front. Small hisses of green gas eked out of it as it rose up, taller than Timmy, on a narrow tendril of shadow.

"*At last*," said Dark Cloud. "*I've found you, boy.*"

CHAPTER 16:

YOU WISH
YOU WERE
TIMMY

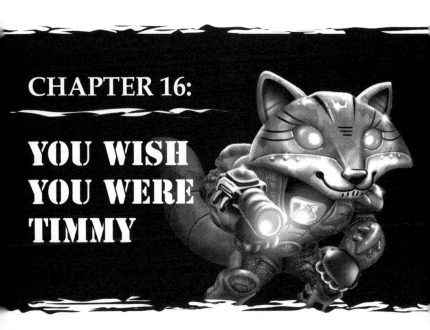

Nimble, being as quick as she was, immediately lifted her flasher and fired off a very fast barrage of blue light. Pilfer was right when he said that the Forest Guard's upgraded flashers were three times faster—the tiny blue balls burst forth like bullets from a machine gun, making a sound like *thoothoothoothoothoothoothoom!*

But Dark Cloud was no fool. He knew the

squirrel was there, and he was ready. Quick as a flash, he dodged to the left and then sank back into the fog, out of sight. Nimble pointed her flasher all around.

"Where'd he go?" she asked quietly. Then, with a small squeak, Nimble vanished, sucked down into the black fog by the Dark.

"Nimble!" Timmy shouted. "Nimble, where did you go?!"

"What *is* that thing?" Ms. Gertrude asked. Her eyes were wide in shock. She was having enough trouble believing that the small silver squirrel was real, and now a shadow with a painted skull for a face had literally appeared out of nowhere.

"That's the Dark," Glen said quickly. "They're like shadows, but they move and talk and try to steal children."

So the reports from the city of shadows

moving all on their own… they were real, Ms. Gertrude thought. *And the talking bears, too.* First she pinched herself hard on the arm to make sure she wasn't dreaming. When she didn't wake up, she sprang into action—which is a phrase that means "started doing something other than standing there, looking shocked."

"Get behind me!" she ordered the two boys. "Whatever this thing is, I'll take care of it. I'm an expert in three martial arts, and was trained by a world-champion in… *whoa!*" Suddenly Ms. Gertrude's foot was yanked out from under her as Dark Cloud's shadowy tendrils pulled her into the fog. She bumped her head on the rough forest floor and was out cold.

Dark Cloud rose from the fog once more, directly in front of Glen and Timmy. There was nothing the two boys could do. If they took another step backwards, they would plunge into the cold river, and the current was very strong. They would certainly get swept away. But they couldn't move forward, either, on account of the tall, skinny shadow hissing green chemicals into the air. This is what some people would refer to as being "stuck between a rock and a hard place," which is a phrase that does not involve literal rocks and hard places, but means that neither of the two options is a very good one.

Dark Cloud looked from one boy to the other. Then he hissed, *"Which one of you is Timmy?"*

The boys just looked at each other for a moment in confusion. As I mentioned before, the Dark had trouble telling one human from another, and they had a lot of trouble telling two different children apart. To make matters worse, Timmy and Glen were both boys, so Dark Cloud had no idea which was which.

Before Timmy could even think to say

anything, Glen raised his hand and said, "Me. I'm Timmy."

"What? No, you're not!" Timmy protested. "*I'm* Timmy." He very much appreciated that Glen was being so brave, but he didn't want anything bad to happen to his friend because of him.

"Ha!" Glen laughed. "You *wish* you were Timmy. It's me, you big ugly shadow. I'm Timmy."

"Don't listen to him," said (the real) Timmy. "His name is Glen. I'm Timmy."

"*Enough!*" Dark Cloud roared. "*I'll just take you both!*" Thin tendrils of shadow shot out of the fog. One of them wrapped around Timmy's arm, and another twirled around Glen's waist. They yanked the boys forward, towards Dark Cloud. "*Your father will open the gate for me, not Total Dark! And the forces of shadow will be under my command!*" The Dark laughed horribly, which sounded like ice cubes being crushed under a heavy boot. He laughed so loudly that he didn't hear the other sound, the one behind him.

Whhhiiiirrrr.... THOOM!

A narrow beam of blue light shot through the air, so bright that for a moment afterwards Timmy saw spots in his vision. The flasher beam struck Dark Cloud right in his shadowy tendril, directly below his chemical-canister head. The light sliced through him like the wing of an airplane cuts through a cloud. The chemical canister fell to the forest floor with a clatter. The tendrils that were wrapped around the boys quickly let go, and what remained of Dark Cloud slithered into the fog as it hissed in pain.

Sneak ran over to the boys. "Are you two okay?" he asked.

"Yeah, I think so," said Timmy. Behind the

orange bear were Patch, Pilfer, Anna, and Sly. "Where are the others? Mother? Blue? Bruiser?"

Patch shook her head. "We didn't find them."

"Everyone, form up," said Sly. "We don't know how many Dark are here in the forest, and they have the fog at their advantage." The four animals formed a line in front of the three children and raised their flashers, waiting for the Dark to show up again.

"Sly," said Pilfer, "do you sense any movement with your motion sensors?"

The fox looked left and right. "Yes… and it's right… over… there!" She pointed her flashers and fired a quick barrage, *thoothoothoothoom!*

A moment later a familiar silver head with lavender eyes popped up from the fog. "Hey, what's the big idea?" said Nimble. She was still a little woozy from the green gas that Dark Cloud had breathed on her, but she was okay—the flashers didn't hurt her because they fired pure light, and as you well know from being out in the sun, light doesn't hurt anything but the Dark (and vampires, of course, but that's a whole different type of story).

"Wait! There's more movement," said Sly. "From over… there!" She turned and fired again. This time it was Ms. Gertrude who appeared in the fog, rubbing the back of her head and looking very disappointed.

"Oh, I was hoping that was all just a bad dream," she grumbled. "Great. Now there's a fox, and a raccoon, and… bears." She narrowed her eyes. There *were* bears, two of them, wearing orange and yellow armor.

"Timmy, who is that woman?" asked Pilfer.

"That's my nanny," said Timmy.

"How in the world did she find us?" Patch asked.

"I'm not sure," said Timmy.

"You know, you could just ask me yourself," Ms. Gertrude complained. "I'm standing right here."

"Hey, guys! Look!" Nimble pointed excitedly in the distance. From between two trees came a familiar shape—someone tall, and made even taller by the antlers on its head.

"It's Stag!" said Pilfer. "Stag, we're over here! Be careful, the Dark are in the forest!"

"Hmm," said Sly. "That's strange. I see him, but my motion sensors aren't picking anything up. It's as if he's not really there at all."

Timmy gasped. He was about to shout that it was a distraction—that it wasn't Stag, but a silhouette of fog made by the Dark—but he didn't get the chance. A tendril of shadow wrapped around his waist and pulled him backwards... not into the forest, but into the river behind him.

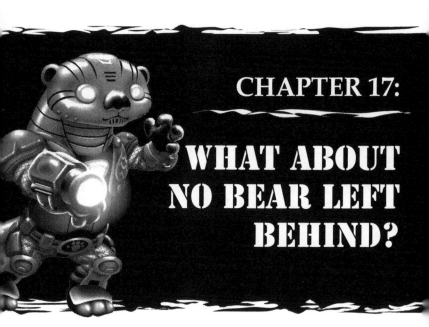

CHAPTER 17:

WHAT ABOUT NO BEAR LEFT BEHIND?

One moment, Timmy was standing on the shore, watching the Stag silhouette get closer. In the next moment, he was yanked off his feet and plunged into the cold water of the river. He was moving very fast as the Dark tugged him deeper and deeper into the water.

"*I told you I'd get you, boy,*" the shadow hissed. Timmy fought and thrashed, but there was nothing he could do to escape. Dark Cloud was trying to pull him all the way across the river to the other side.

And then a truly horrible thought crossed Timmy's mind: did the Dark know that humans couldn't breathe underwater? Would he drown before they reached the other shore?

He tried to say something, to shout, "I can't breathe!" but it came out as gurgles and glugs. He couldn't even tell which way was up; all he saw around him was dark blue and black.

"*I hope your bear friends can swim!*" The Dark laughed its terrible laugh again.

Suddenly a shape swam by, right in front of Timmy's face. Was it another Dark? He couldn't tell, it moved so fast through the water. But a moment later, he got his answer.

A beam of blue light sliced through the water and struck the shadowy tentacles that were holding onto Timmy. The Dark screeched and howled. Then came a quick burst of tiny blue balls, punching holes in the shadow.

"*Aaarrgh!*" Dark Cloud shrieked. The tendril around Timmy's waist loosened, and the last thing Timmy saw of the Dark was a tiny, thin shred of shadow swimming away, like a skinny black serpent wriggling through the water.

A pair of hands grabbed onto him. They were small hands, but they were strong, and they pulled him up, up, and through the surface of the river. Timmy took a deep, gasping breath of air as the small, strong hands pulled him towards the shore.

"It's okay," said a high-pitched voice over his shoulder. "I've got you."

Back on dry land, Timmy dripped water and coughed as Sneak and Patch and Anna hurried over to make sure he was alright.

"I'm okay," he said weakly, still coughing on river water. "I'm okay, thanks to…" He turned to see who had saved him, and was only a little surprised to see a small red armored otter.

"The name's Boxer," said the otter. "Of the River Patrol. Nice to see you again, Timmy. Sorry you're all wet."

"An otter," grumbled Ms. Gertrude. "Now there's an otter."

"Aww, he's adorable!" Anna gushed.

"I ain't adorable! I'm fierce," said the small otter in his high-pitched voice. "Say, what's with this strange fog?"

Timmy looked around. Curiously, the fog seemed to be rising again. But instead of the low, dense, black fog it had been a moment before, it was like it was spreading out, becoming a thick, dark gray mist.

"That Dark, the one in the river, he must

have been controlling the fog," said Sly. "Did you get him, Boxer?"

The otter shook his head. "Not all of 'im. A little piece went slithering away like a worm."

"Well," said Pilfer, "don't you worry about that. The Forest Guard will take care of whatever's left."

"And you, Timmy," said Nimble, "have to go on now."

"What?" Timmy was terribly confused. "I thought we were going to wait for the others."

"There's no time," said Sly. "The Dark are in the forest. Every moment that we sit here waiting is another chance for them to get to you. The River Patrol is here. You have to keep moving."

"I only see an otter," said Anna.

"Well, you ain't lookin' hard enough, are you?" Boxer pointed towards the river. From out of the dark gray mist came a shape… quite a large one, in fact, floating in the river like a huge piece of driftwood. As it got closer, its purple eyes glowed brightly and its huge tail swished slowly back and forth.

"Is that an… alligator?" Glen asked.

"Sure is," said Boxer. On the alligator's back were a blue turtle and a small green frog. There was something else, too—the alligator was pulling along a raft behind it, made of wood, and sitting on the raft was a small orange beaver with huge front teeth.

The raft reminded Timmy of a tree fort that he and his dad had built when they lived at the edge of the forest. In fact, it looked *very* similar to the tree fort he and his dad had built. Timmy wondered if it could be the same one.

"All aboard who's comin' aboard!" said Boxer, and then the otter leaped into the river.

"No," said Timmy, shaking his head. "No,

we have to wait for Mother and Blue and Bruiser. We can't go on without them. Tell them, Sneak."

The orange bear sighed and squeezed Timmy's shoulder. "I'm sorry, Timmy. If Mother was here, she would tell us that we had to go on."

"But…" He couldn't believe what he was hearing. Tears stung at the corners of his eyes. "What about no bear left behind?"

"Hey." Nimble hopped over and balanced on her thick silver tail. "Listen to me. The rest of Bear Company is in these woods somewhere, and the Forest Guard will make it our number-one duty to find them and send them your way. We promise."

"Yeah," said Pilfer. "Mother is very resourceful. She'll find her way back to you, I just know it."

Timmy shook his head again. He wasn't going to move. He would stay right there, in that spot, until Mother and the others came. But then Anna reached out and she took his hand in hers. "Come on, Timmy," she said quietly. Suddenly his legs were moving, slowly, and the next thing he knew he had stepped out onto the wooden raft.

"Hey, Sneak." Sly unclipped the upgraded flasher from her wrist, the solar flare, and held it out to the orange bear. "Swap with me."

"Huh? Why?" said Sneak.

"I think you'll need the upgrade more than I will."

Sneak nodded and switched out the flasher. "Thank you," he said. "Please, find the others for us."

"We will," Sly promised. Pilfer traded his flasher with Patch, and the two bears got onto the raft.

But Glen hadn't yet moved from the riverbank.

"Glen?" said Timmy. "Aren't you coming?"

"I don't think so," the boy said. "It's been a lot of fun, but I have to find my family. I think I should head home and stay put until they come back. They're probably really worried."

"I'll take you home," said Ms. Gertrude. Just about everyone had forgotten that she was there. "My car is parked at the farm, so I have to go back there anyway."

"Does that mean you're going to stop following me?" Timmy asked.

For the first time ever, Ms. Gertrude smiled at Timmy. "No," she said. "It just means I'm giving you a little bit of a head start."

Considering everything you know about Ms. Gertrude, this might seem a little strange—she finally had Timmy right there in front of her and was letting him go again. But you see, everything that Ms. Gertrude thought she knew for certain was now wrong; there *were* talking bears, and foxes and squirrels and otters, too. And there *were* shadows that moved all on their own and tried to steal children.

What you don't know is that when Timmy was pulled into the water, all of the members of the Dark Corps were looking at the river, wondering where he had gone. No one was looking at Ms. Gertrude, so she took out her cell phone and took a picture of the strange armored animals. Her plan now was to take it back to her agency and show it to them so that they knew what they were up against. She had no idea how to deal with this on her own… and there was still the matter of the rookie agent who was heading her way, the one named Reese who claimed to know a thing or two about what was going on.

Ms. Gertrude was still going to get to the bottom of this, and she was still going to get

Timmy Barnes back before he could reach his dad. Because what Timmy didn't know, but Ms. Gertrude *did* know, was that Timmy still had a long, long way to go before he reached the secret Arctic base where his father was being kept.

So she smiled, and she waved, and she promised to help Glen get back to his family.

The large green alligator shoved off from the shore and swam back out onto the river, pulling the big wooden raft behind him slowly. The red otter, Boxer, swam behind the raft, occasionally diving down beneath it to make sure that none of the Dark were in the water.

Sly, Pilfer, Nimble, and Glen all waved as Timmy, Anna, Patch, and Sneak headed out on the next part of their journey.

"Do you really think the others will catch up to us?" Timmy asked.

"I'm sure of it," said Sneak.

"Definitely. Nothing to worry about," said Patch.

Timmy didn't feel like either of them was very sure about it.

CHAPTER 18:

TAKING OVER

Stupid forest," Bruiser grumbled. "Stupid fog, stupid river…" He was terribly lost. Even though Bruiser would never admit it, he had an awful sense of direction. He had no idea which way the river was. To make matters worse, the thick black fog had turned into a grayish mist that covered everything, from the forest floor up to the highest branches, as thick as the smoke from a wildfire. He couldn't see more than a few feet in front of him.

At the same time, Dark Cloud slithered over rocks and between trees. He had escaped from the river, even if barely. It wasn't even really fair to call him Dark Cloud anymore, because he was little more than a tiny sliver of a shadow. The bears and their friends had beaten him yet again. To make matters worse, he had lost control of his fog. Parts of his shadow were still bonded with it, but he could barely feel it now, and it was spreading along all on its own, as gases tend to do, and going where it pleased. He had no idea how he could recover from this. He would have to find some very weak Dark to absorb, and there weren't any Dark around there. When the sun came up again, he was sure he would evaporate forever.

Dark Cloud was so distracted by his

thoughts that he didn't even notice the green bear, stumbling alone through the forest, until he had run right into it.

"What was that?!" Bruiser shouted as he jumped back, his flasher raised. "I felt something! I know I did! Come out where I can see you, and I'll tear you apart!"

Dark Cloud slithered quickly behind a tree. If the bear saw him, it would easily blast him into nothing. He had to escape. He had to run away, and get to somewhere safe...

Wait, Dark Cloud thought. He peeked out from behind the tree and saw that this bear had a crack in its armor, right over its plushy belly.

I'm sure you remember earlier when I said that Dark Cloud was very resourceful and clever. He was too weak to bond with a bear—he had tried it with Sneak and failed. He was too weak to fight the bear—he had tried that too and failed.

But maybe there was another way.

"Come on out!" Bruiser shouted. "I don't care if there's one of you or a thousand of you! I'll take you all on!"

Dark Cloud slithered quickly towards the bear like a snake in the grass. He wriggled up the bear's leg, around its belly, and then slipped right into the crack in Bruiser's armor.

"Hey!" said Bruiser. "What is that? What are you doing? Knock it off!" Bruiser squirmed and flailed around, but there was nothing he could do about the tiny Dark that had made its way inside his armor.

Now I'm sure you know that the most important part of a human is our brain. It controls everything that we say and do, and all the things we don't have to think about doing, like breathing and blinking and keeping our heart beating and our blood pumping. Even a computer has a brain, or something like it, and much like humans, it's a very small part of a much larger machine.

Bruiser was no different. Inside the metal case on his back was his "brain," which was a powerful microprocessor invented by Dr. Barnes that made him walk and talk and grumble and fight the Dark. Of course, Dark Cloud didn't know anything about brains or computers or microprocessors, but he did know that if he slithered around inside Bruiser long enough, he might find something important.

Dark Cloud squeezed himself as flat as he could and wriggled into the metal case on Bruiser's back. He found the microprocessor, and decided that it looked very important. It was quite small—the perfect size for him to bond with.

Poor Bruiser didn't know what to do. One moment he was squirming and flailing, and the next he was…

Well, there's no easy way to say this. He wasn't Bruiser anymore.

Dark Cloud looked down at his small hands. He moved his arms, and then his legs. He felt very strange—he had never had a real body before. It was strange, but it was also wonderful. He had a light weapon on his wrist, and green armor, and a bear body.

He had done it. He had bonded with a bear.

Now he could become the most powerful Dark that ever lived. He could overtake Total Dark. He could command the forces of the shadows, and not even the sun could stop him.

But first, he decided, he would find the other four.

END
OF
BOOK FOUR

THE
DARK CRPS
ADVENTURES
will continue in more exciting books!

Featuring...

BEAR COMPANY

WOLF SQUAD

AIR STRIKE

HOMESTEAD DEFENSE FORCE

CORPS COMMAND

JUNGLE BRIGADE

FOREST GUARD

ARMOR DIVISION

RIVER PATROL

DARK OPS

DESERT TROOP

ALPINE RANGERS

WINTER WATCH

NEVER BE AFRAID OF THE DARK

WWW.DARKCORPS.COM

About the Author

Cameron Alexander is the pen name of a mysterious wizard from a different time and a different world. Search for him if you can and if you find him, let me know. He owes me 10 dollars.

www.bickeringowls.com

14219820R00106

Made in the USA
Middletown, DE
19 November 2018